DEATHLESS

ANNALS OF THE GOD EATER BOOK 1

THE GOD EATER SAGA

ROB J. HAYES

A NOTE FROM THE AUTHOR

Time for a little info on format. DEATHLESS is book 1 of the Annals of the God Eater trilogy, and also part of the larger God Eater Saga which will consist of 9 books.

The God Eater Saga is a trilogy of trilogies being written and released concurrently. That means I wrote all 3 book 1s at the same time and I'm releasing them together. I've also started writing all 3 book 2s and will be releasing them together as well. I know, it's a strange way to do things, but bear with me.

Writing and releasing the saga this way allows me to weave mysteries, reveals, world building, and character development across the 9 books and across 3000 years of in world history. I felt it was important to do it this way because many of the characters in God Eater are immortals and have been alive a LONG time.

But fear not! Each trilogy is designed to work on its own as well. If you just want know how the Godless Kings waged war on Heaven (ANNALS OF THE GOD EATER), that's fine, you'll get all the pertinent information you need within those pages. But if you choose to read the full saga (AGE OF THE GOD EATER, ANNALS OF THE GOD EATER, ARCHIVE OF THE GOD EATER), you'll get a much deeper understanding of the world and the story. And there may be some reveals in the past that shine a new light on events in the present.

For ease of understanding when all 3 trilogies take place, here's a handy little summary:

<u>Age of the God Eater</u> (main series)
    Herald (book 1)

<u>Annals of the God Eater</u> (set 1000 years before Herald)
    Deathless (book 1)

<u>Archive of the God Eater</u> (set 3000 years before Herald)
    Demon (book 1)

I know it all sounds a little confusing. Believe me, it was certainly a headache keeping it all straight in my head. But I can assure you it will all make sense in the end.

THANK YOU for reading, and I do hope you check out all 3 trilogies to get the best understanding of the world.

Rob

CHAPTER I

King Ertide Hostain stared down at the handkerchief spotted bright red with his blood. His chest burned. His ribs were too tight crushing his heart. His breath rasped in his throat as he fought for air. His vision danced, swam, flared bright and then dimmed. He was dying.

The door to his quarters opened and the clamour of servants outside flooded in. Jertis, his manservant, strode inside and closed the door behind him.

"Heaven's Light, sire," the whip crack of a man sketched an informal bow, then quickly set about cleaning up the clutter of the previous night's festivities.

Ertide stifled another cough, wiped the last spots of blood from his lips, then crushed the handkerchief in his fist. He couldn't let anyone see, they couldn't know. Not even Jertis. The merest hint of infirmity and the wolves would circle, ready to pick apart his corpse and everything he had built with it.

He had yet to choose an heir. It had simply never seemed important. He had never truly felt old before. But it was a decision he would have to make soon before the choice was taken away from him. If the angels had their way, he had no doubt they'd put Caran on the throne after he was gone, and then what would happen to the empire? Ertide loved his third son, but he had never liked him. Caran was a pious, bureaucratic lickspittle. The throne needed iron, a ruler willing to stand up to divine *requests*, or at the very least someone smart enough to circumvent them. Sometimes Ertide felt he had been doing that his entire life. He sometimes remembered a younger man, a man known as the Crimson Prince, who had rode into battle, cut down enemies, protected the empire's borders. So long ago the memories felt more like stories he had once heard.

Ertide glanced down at the bloody scrap of cloth crushed in his fist. *Surely God must already know of my illness. He sees all, knows all. Doesn't he?*

Ertide crossed to the fire and threw his bloody handkerchief to the flames, watching the fabric flare and burn away. "What's on the cards today, Jertis?"

Jertis cleared his throat pointedly. "Well first, sire, I suggest a change of clothing." The man was busying himself in the bedchamber, tidying things away, laying out a dark green suit and black britches. "I would normally suggest a bath, too, but it's already mid-morning."

"God's Breath, it is?" Ertide shook his head. He'd had a lot to drink last night. It was Ylnaea's fault. Bloody woman was too young for him by half, but the king needed a queen and she was determined to give him one more son before he became too old to try.

Jertis crossed into the living chamber, a slight smile on his lips. He threw open the curtains and bright light streamed in, dazzling Ertide.

"Is it really so late?" Ertide said. "That woman will be the death of me, Jertis."

"Yes, sire."

Jertis busied himself about while Ertide moved into the bedchambers and stripped from yesterday's clothes and into the fresh suit. It was new, he realised. Slimmer than he was used to, better suited to his frame as he wasted away with old age. He opened his wardrobe to find all his clothes were new. *When did that happen?* Damn, Jertis knew him better than he knew himself.

Ertide glanced at himself in the mirror. He'd always been tall, but now we had a slight stoop. He hadn't swung a sword in years and that was starting to show in his shoulders and arms. His skin sagged around his jowls and had lost much of its vibrancy. The healthy brown quickly turning a dull, dusty shade. It all seemed to be happening so quickly, as though age were a snake he'd run from all his life, but it had snuck up on him and now it was constricting him tighter and tighter.

Jertis let in the servants and they brought food and breakfast wine. Ertide ate quickly, quail eggs with brown toast. There were fruits, pastries, bacon, preserves. He ignored them all. He didn't have the appetite he used to, and the pastries were too rich for him these days, as like to upset his stomach as not. Not that he would tell anyone that. He missed them, truth be told. Missed the feeling of soft pastry flaking away in his mouth, and sweet preserve setting his tongue alight. But they weren't worth the burning acid in his stomach.

"The cards, Jertis?" Ertide asked as he ate.

"There's a delegation from the Ice Isles, requesting new terms on the trade deals for leviathan oil."

Ertide gave a noncommittal grunt. The Ice Walkers were always after better terms. He'd have marched a few legions up there and made the land part of the empire if they had any actual lands to secure. But the ice was made of thousands of floating islands and only the Ice Walkers knew how to traverse it safely. Previous kings had tried to take the isles, and previous kings had left a legacy of failure. Ertide would not fail.

"Architects have arrived from Everheim to discuss the restoration of the Grand Samir courtyard."

Ertide pushed aside his plate, his appetite fled. The Grand Samir Courtyard had long ago fallen into disrepair. They'd once used it to stage plays and poetry recitals, but the Third Age had ended and with it had gone the need for such luxuries. They were living in the Fourth Age now and the focus had shifted. A decree from Heaven, from God himself, delivered by his winged servants. *A decree I could not refuse.* They were living in the Age of Exploration now, and he'd since spent half his life diverting funds and workers to building ships and supplying expeditions that never returned. Whatever lay beyond the borders of the Sant Dien Empire was apparently quite dangerous.

"What's this?" Ertide asked. There was a white paper half hidden under a pastry.

"A note from Prince Rikkan, sire," Jertis said.

Ertide broke the seal on the note and opened it. It was his son's handwriting, messy and rushed. Just like Rikkan, if it didn't have a blade on the end, he cared little for learning it. Ertide had despaired over his penmanship many times, but his eldest son didn't care and was as stubborn as a pegasus.

The letter contained only two words.

'He's here.'

Ertide could feel his son's frustration through the ink. He crushed the note, more fuel for the fire. *Stupid man, writing it down.* But then words were just as dangerous spoken as written. The God was everywhere, saw everything, knew everything.

Only the thoughts in my head are sacred. Those at least, he was certain the God did not know. If he did, he'd have had Ertide's crown removed long ago.

Jertis continued with his list. Union bosses from the maintenance guild to discuss the pilgrimage paths up to the Overlook. An ambassador from Aelegar no doubt to claim innocence over recent banditry in the south. A request from the Deepwater Exploring company to part fund an expedition into the caverns beneath the Cinderspire. At no point did the man mention the Rider, but Ertide knew Rikkan would not lie. The Herald of the Fourth Age was here, and he would no doubt bring new holy demands.

CHAPTER 2

Arandon was waiting for Ertide outside his quarters. His grandson was a slight man, with the Hostain height, but none of the brawn. He was chubby around the cheeks and neck, and his skin was so light he was almost pale. He was also immaculately groomed in the flowing red robe of a scholar, with a dark beard and hair neatly trimmed. He sat on a richly embroidered chair, staring down at the notes he kept on his wooden carry board. He carried that board everywhere, his various notes always close at hand.

"Heaven's Light, Grandfather," Arandon said cheerily.

"Heaven's Light," Ertide grumbled. He hated that greeting, a daily reminder that each and every day was a blessing from the God.

Arandon stood and fell in beside Ertide as he strode down the corridor. A servant immediately rushed forward and picked up the chair, carrying it behind them a few paces in case Arandon should want to sit down again. Such opulence made the man soft in the body, pudgy. It was small wonder that Rikkan found his son so disappointing. But Ertide knew better. Men like Arandon were not meant for combat with blades, but for battles of the mind.

"We missed you at morning prayers, Grandfather," Arandon said cagily.

And no doubt my pious wife will flog me for it later, even though it's at least mostly her fault. A dull pounding ache above his left eye was proof enough she was to blame. *Was it two bottles of wine, or three? Bloody woman could out drink a whole platoon of soldiers.*

"Number of leagues between Celesgarde and Vael?" Ertide asked.

Arandon smiled at the game and was silent for a moment, calculating. "One hundred and forty-two."

"By road?"

"As the hawk flies."

Ertide chuckled. "One hundred and fifty-two. Check it."

Arandon struggled to keep up with Ertide as he thumbed through his papers searching for the correct page. Servants bowed and backed out of the way at their passing, others trailing behind. Soldiers of the First Legion, the palace guard, stood to attention at every intersection, they wore plated armour painted black with a single stripe of gold down the chest plate. They were pointless really, nobody had broken into the palace in decades, but the semblance of order was good to keep people in line. Almost as good as the fear of God.

"Shit!" Arandon said. "You're right, Grandfather. Though I'm really not sure why I say that with surprise. How do you know it all?"

Ertide just smiled. His grandson didn't need to know that he looked up these facts each morning to make certain he knew the answer to whatever quiz he fired off.

"Angel to Castle five, capturing Bandit," Ertide said. They'd been playing games like this for years, the entire board played out only in their minds. A true test of memory and strategy. Arandon was the only person Ertide knew who could beat him at games of Clash, he had such a keen mind.

"Hmmm," Arandon said. He cocked his head to the side slightly as he considered. "Wulfkin to Exemplar Three, slaying Eagle."

Ertide laughed. "A bold play, but you leave your right flank open. Pegasus to Demon four. I think you'll find your Reaver is about to fall, and the third shrine will soon be mine."

Arandon frowned at that, then shook his head. "I took your Pegasus twelve moves back, Grandfather."

A moment of panic shot through Ertide, but he didn't break his stride, didn't let the confusion show. He just laughed to hide it. "Sharp as ever, lad."

"You knew? Of course you knew. Always testing me." He flicked through his notes. "You almost had me doubting myself this time. But no, see." He tapped at the board, showing a sheet of paper with the game board and all their moves noted upon it.

Ertide raised an eyebrow as he quickly studied the positions of their pieces, memorising them. "Making notes defeats the point, Arandon," he said. "It's cheating."

Arandon quickly covered the sheet over with his other notes. "I... yes. Sorry, Grandfather. I'll pay penance tonight. A sacrifice for my falsity."

Ertide stopped and took his grandson by the shoulders. He was only just a man, far too young to be concerning himself with sacrifices he couldn't afford. Besides, he shouldn't have to sacrifice anything to God when it was Ertide he had wronged.

"No need for any of that, Arandon. We sacrifice enough, more than enough, every day. It's only a game. Your apology is penance enough for me." He winked and clapped his grandson on the shoulder, then moved on. By the weighted silence behind him, he wagered his words had not mollified the lad.

What will he sacrifice tonight on the altar of God's approval? For a crime that should be mine to judge, not Heaven's.

They strode on, turning a corner and down a staircase to the lowest level of the palace. Arandon had wit, the intelligence and the cunning to be a good leader, but he lacked courage, conviction. And he was prone to cheating to get his way, then quick to apologise when he was caught. And he was too pious by far. Arandon would never have the spine to stand up to the angels, he would forever capitulate and call it compromise.

At the bottom of the staircase was a wild ruckus. Arandon's eldest siblings, the twins, were busy creating a scene. Emrik and Merian brought a life and joy and energy to the palace that made Ertide's spirits soar. They were both long past childhood, with children of their own now, and yet they still acted the fools whenever they were together. Emrik had Merian's daughter, Urtrid, on his shoulders, and Merian had Emrik's son, Conran, similarly hoisted. They charged at each other, crying braying noises, while the children slapped at each other at every pass, giggling with glee all the while.

Ertide waited until the next pass, then hurried across the foyer floor to get out of the way. Arandon and their entourage of servants followed quickly.

"Care to make a wager, Grandfather?" Emrik yelled, grinning wildly. "I say Conran has the better steed, but Urtrid has a slap that could bring down a wulfkin."

"Pah!" Merian bellowed. "Such ignorant flattery. What do we say, Conran?"

The toddler atop Merian's shoulders flailed his arms in the air and squealed. "CHARGE!" Merian lurched into a canter, and opposite her Emrik did the same. They passed each other, snorting, and the two children slapped each others' hands.

"Too close to call," Ertide called as the twins circled around for another pass. "Good hunting to you both."

"What do you say to the king?" Emrik said, jiggling Urtrid atop his shoulders.

The girl pulled a face of fierce concentration, then smiled wide. "I want the crown."

Emrik burst out laughing, but Merian had the graces to look aghast. She shouted an apology for her daughter, but Ertide just waved it away as he strode on.

Arandon smoldered beside him. "God's Breath, grow up," he muttered.

"Forgive them their frivolity, Arandon. Let them enjoy their lives."

"Hmph! I've been forgiving them that my entire life, yet they still get to run around without a care while I had to bear the brunt of..." He stopped and cleared his throat. "Sorry, Grandfather. I only wish they would take on some responsibility. For the good of the empire, to see God's will done."

The palace was a titanic building with seven circular and domed wings spread out around the central structure. Each of the wings was home to a branch of the Hostain family. An expansive dynasty under one roof. As king, Ertide spent most of his time only in the central building. It was the responsibility of others to come to him. But sometimes he grew bored with meeting with people in the throne room or his study. Besides, nothing threw people off their rehearsed speeches quite like a change in locale.

"I think we'll do this in the arboretum today," he declared as he marched towards the palace doors and out into the blazing mid-morning light.

He had to hold up a hand to shield his eyes while they adjusted, one more thing that was taking longer these days. Gravel crunched under foot and the smell of leather and horses assaulted him.

How long has it been since I last ventured out for a hunt? Years?

A carriage had pulled up and as the door opened, a portly woman in a dazzling array of furs stepped down. She had colourful tattoos scrawled all over her face and hands, and probably elsewhere, too. A Lorekeeper from the Ice Islands, then. That meant the Ice Walkers meant to remind him of some bit of obscure history while they made their case.

The woman startled when she saw the king and immediately went down onto one knee on the gravel.

"Sun protect you from the ice, King Ertide," the Lorekeeper purred.

"Heaven's Light is all the protection we need from the ice and anything lurking beneath it," Arandon said.

Ertide gave her a brief greeting, then moved on. He waved Arandon to his side as he walked.

"When am I meeting the Ice Walkers?"

Arandon glanced down at the daily schedule. "Third meeting of the day."

"Send to Arkenhold University for a historian. I have no intention of being blindsided by that woman and her wandering tattoos. So much history they claim to keep, but how are we to know what is true and false?"

In truth, he envied the Ice Walkers a little. They were both part of the Sant Dien Empire, and also not. They did not worship the God, but instead the ice and the sun that kept them safe from its freezing embrace. And yet, the God had never ordered Ertide or any of his ancestors to stamp out that false faith. Not since the Shattering had an army marched on the ice, and that had been to throw back the demons from the depths, to save the Ice Walkers, not subjugate them.

The arboretum was not far and it was a glorious day for a stroll. Winter was failing, losing its grip, while spring was beginning to claw its way back to dominance. The grounds were starting to erupt in verdant bloom. Over a dozen gardeners were busy keeping the flower beds tended and weeded, including Ertide's youngest sister, Flury.

She pushed a chord of dark hair over her shoulder and waved a gloved hand. "Heaven's Light, brother. What a glorious day we're in for, not a cloud in the sky."

Ertide waved back. Flury Hostain had spent her whole life tending the palace gardens. She'd never married, took no part in court politics or the empire's rule. She had never even left the capital as far as Ertide was aware. He couldn't imagine leading such a cloistered existence. Even now, old and weary, he champed at the bit to ride out and see more of his empire. It had been... years now since he had last found a good excuse to get away.

An angel swooped overhead, wings beating, robes fluttering. She banked hard, swept around in a gust of wind, and alighted on the gravel just a few paces from Ertide. If any human had approached him at such speed, his guards would have rushed forward to protect him, but not from an angel. So well trained they were to think of the winged folk as their allies. As their betters even.

We bow and scrape where we should bristle and guard.

Oronesus, the Bookkeeper, was an angel of the Fourth Age. Like all her kin, she was immortal, but she was also young. The Fourth Age was only thirty years old, so that meant she was younger than some of Ertide's children. And yet, Oronesus was a wondrous woman to look upon no matter how many times Ertide saw her. She was a full head taller than him, making her a giant by any but Aelegar standards. Her skin was a deep brown, darker than Ertide's own, and her hair was black as pitch. Auburn wings, like a hawk's, couched high on her back, the feathers mesmerising to look at. She took his breath away, no matter how many times he saw her. By the awed silence behind him, Ertide knew he was not alone in that bedazzlement.

Strained silence stretched between them. *I will not bow, nor scrape. I am king here.*

Oronesus shook out her wings and pulled around the satchel on her hip, bulging with tomes. Ertide heard scraping behind him as the others went down on one knee. Even Arandon lowered himself. Only he and Oronesus remained standing. He met her gaze and saw her brown eyes turn golden, and he knew he had pushed it as far as he could.

God is watching.

With a pained groan, Ertide lowered himself to one knee. And hated himself for it. *I should not have to bow to her, or to anyone.* But Oronesus was a child of the God. She served the God, as did they all. *We serve at his whim and his sufferance.*

"Heaven's Light, Bookkeeper," Ertide said.

"Stand, Ertide," Oronesus said, her voice soft and hazy as flowing smoke. She held out her hands to him and he let her pull him to his feet. Her grip was iron, stronger than even Rikkan's crushing paws. "You are king. You have no need to bow to me."

Ertide met her gaze and saw her eyes had returned to their normal fathomless brown. "Forgive me, Bookkeeper," he said breathlessly. "I was rather taken aback by your grand entrance."

Oronesus laughed and Ertide found a smile pulling at his own lips despite himself. Angels often had that effect on people, pulling on their emotions.

"We missed you at morning prayers," the angel said.

"I, uh... Overslept. The queen kept me up late."

Oronesus laughed again, even more deeply this time. "You'll have to make up for it with the evening sacrifice."

Ertide slammed on a smile of his own and hoped it didn't look too much like a grimace. "Of course."

"I was waiting for you in the throne room," Oronesus said.

"Yes." Ertide waved towards the arboretum, he spoke through his teeth. "I thought, for a change, I... We could hold court somewhere different. Ylnaea says the cacti are in flower and are spectacular."

Oronesus gave an appreciative nod. "A wonderful idea. To see God's will in bloom. I approve."

I didn't ask for your approval.

"And how is Ylnaea?" Oronesus asked as they walked. She made it sound so innocent.

Don't worry, she's keeping me pious. Not to mention she's voracious enough I'm certain she's trying to screw me to death. The angels had been the ones to push Ertide into remarrying after Giliana had died, and they had also been the ones to choose his new wife. Few people were as pious as Ylnaea, and he had no doubt she reported to the angels daily.

"She's well," Ertide hedged.

"Not with child yet?" Oronesus asked.

Ertide ground his teeth. "I fear I may be too old to give her that."

They reached the arboretum and Ertide flicked his hand. Jertis hurried forward and pulled open the door. Oronesus was the first through, striding on before he had the chance.

King in name. Servant in practice.

CHAPTER 3

THE FIRST MEETING FOR THE DAY WAS THE ARCHITECTS FROM Everheim in the east, where the Collegium held sway. It was said each and every student of the Collegium had apprenticed under Armstar, the Builder, himself. Many of those students were still funnelled into that useless bloody tower the angel was set on constructing. It was a waste of time and manpower, and most importantly, funds. Ertide had been syphoning resources away from the project for decades now, leaving it manned by a skeleton crew barely capable of maintaining the horrific construction. The Builder was not pleased, but he was an artist and the age of artists was over. His word held less weight than other angels these days.

The architects arrived with schematics and drawings and sheets of notes on hand. None of them had thought to bring a mobile document stand like Arandon though. Ertide capitalised on that fact by taking a brisk stroll through the arboretum as he met with the architects, not letting them show him their scrolls.

They were all very complimentary of the palace and its grounds and how the design evoked a feeling of natural wonder like one might find in the turtle shells from the southern Ashlands. The fools thought to butter Ertide like toast before taking a bite. He stopped before a broad, squat tree with a trunk carpeted in emerald moss. Two of the architects stopped to fish scrolls out of their packs, while the lead woman, Architect Mauld, cleared her throat and launched into the pitch.

"Damage to the courtyard grounds was quite extensive. The fire, last Fenswater, was it?" Architect Mauld said.

Arandon flipped a couple of pages to check his notes. "The second Mournsday of Fenswater just gone. One hundred and twelve days ago."

The architect tutted. "The fire gutted much of the infrastructure and the grounds have been left unattended for so long, the entire courtyard will have to be stripped and re-plotted before any building can commence."

Ertide pressed his palm against the moss. It was soft and spongy and slightly moist to the touch. A many-legged insect crawled out of the growth and scuttled across his gnarled finger. "That sounds quite expensive." Before she could answer, he turned and strode away, leaving her two assistants fumbling with the scrolls they had been unrolling to show him.

"Uhh, well, yes," Architect Mauld said as she hurried to catch up, keeping a step behind Ertide as was only proper. "It will certainly not be cheap. But we have drawn up a number of designs for the new courtyard, and our people are ready to work. All we require is for you to choose a design, my king, and..."

"And pay for the work," Ertide said coldly. He felt a sharp pain in his chest that threatened to erupt into another bloody cough, so he slowed down and swallowed the cough into a pointed clearing of his throat.

They were standing just before the cacti, purple and yellow flowers in a riot of bloom. Ylnaea was right, they were breathtaking.

"We have, um..." the architect waved her assistants forward who shuffled on, fiddling with their scrolls.

Ertide held up a hand to forestall them. "Cost?"

The woman swallowed. "Four thousand five hundred sorens, sire."

A bloody fortune. No wonder the treasury is stretched so thin.

Ertide glanced at Arandon. His grandson pulled an incredulous face and shook his head.

This was the truth of Ertide's reign. He'd spent some of his earlier years making war with the barbarians from Aelegar, forging new peace treaties with the Ice Walkers, but most of his three decades on the throne had been spent counting coins and desperately trying to rub two sorens together to force them to breed. After a thousand years of funding art and poetry and extravagant museums, playhouses, and so-called wonders, the empire was already all but beggared. That was the legacy his father and their ancestors had left them. Now, after thirty years of constructing ships and funding expeditions, Ertide had only compounded the issue. There was no end to those with their hands held out for a few coins, and no relief.

Damn my fool of a father. If he had stood his ground just once in his life.

"I thank you for you time, Architect Mauld…"

"When can you begin?" Oronesus asked, her voice the hazy rasp of silken sheets.

"Uh…" The architect glanced between king and angel, then turned to Oronesus.

Sensing where the true power lies.

"We would need to settle on a design." She waved to her assistants again and they surged forward, waving scrolls at the angel. "And many of our workers will need to be pulled from the construction of Star Reach."

Oronesus laughed warmly and raised a hand. The satchel at her hip twitched, the flap folding aside. One of her many tomes floated up out of the satchel and twisted through the air in front of her, the cover creaking open and pages fluttering as though in a breeze. Ertide saw Arandon staring with hungry eyes. He had spoken many times of his jealousy over Oronesus' power over books and paper.

"I will leave the choice of designs up to King Ertide," Oronesus said. The pages of her book stopped fluttering and she ran a slender finger across the page, her eyes roving across whatever was written there.

How gracious of you. Ertide plastered on a grateful smile he didn't feel.

"Rest assured," Oronesus continued. "The restoration of the palace grounds are of utmost importance. You will receive the funds soon."

"Oh yes?" Ertide said. "And will Heaven be opening its coffers?"

The smile Oronesus turned on Ertide sent a chill through his bowels. He sensed he had gone too far. There could be no division between Heaven and the empire. They were one and the same. All they did was to serve God. The crown was but the human arm of God's will.

"I see here there are funds designated to the restoration of Rorash. That fortress has been all but abandoned."

And the restoration of it is important to keep the Aelegar savages in line.

"Have the designs sent to my study," Ertide said, holding out his hand. "I will choose one and get back to you." He wondered if he could syphon more coin away from Star Reach instead.

Architect Mauld grasped his hand. "Heaven's Light go with you, sire."

Ertide gave the briefest smile that quickly curdled. "And with you, Architect."

The woman turned and scuttled away with her assistants, secure in the knowledge the Collegium had just received new funding for at least three years.

The rest of the day passed in much the same way. Whether it was the Ice Walkers wanting new terms, or the Deepwater Guild wanting funds for their foolhardy expedition into the caverns, it was always asking for money. Coins the treasury didn't have and yet whenever Ertide tried to shut the request down, Oronesus undermined him. The angel either had no concept of limitations of the economy, or she didn't care. And of course, no help from Heaven was ever offered. They served God, not the other way around.

Ertide wondered what Heaven looked like. He'd been to the city of Hope up in the north, of course, he'd looked upon Heaven's Gate, the bright light shining down from the sky even at night, illuminating the glowing archway, carved with such reliefs that made the mind boggle. That archway told the history of the empire and of Heaven, and it was forever changing to tell more of their story. But he'd never been allowed through the gate. No human alive had ever been allowed through. He desperately wanted to know what was on the other side. He'd spent his whole life serving God, often willingly, sometimes not, and yet, even he, the king had never seen God's face. Had never heard his voice.

In his darkest times, and always alone, Ertide sometimes wondered if God was even real. Or was he just some fiction conjured by the angels to shackle humanity to their cause? Even to question it was blasphemy, but he needed to know. One way or another, he had to know the truth before he died. Was there truly anyone on the other side of Heaven's Gate? Was his fear of being watched all in vain?

I am a rebellion one man strong, and only in my own mind. Too scared of reprisal to give voice or action to my resistance.

The sun was close to setting by the time the last meeting of the day materialised. The one Rikkan had warned Ertide was coming. Thunder rumbled overhead and the blue sky brightened just for a moment as lightning flashed. The Rider had come.

They were sitting in the orchard square, branches dangling overhead, some heavy with fruit. Polapen, the Bloom Warden, visited the arboretum often and took great pride in bringing the trees to fruit year round regardless of weather outside. He strode around them now, shuffling his oak brown wings and occasionally snapping off twigs or fretting over discoloured leaves. The angel never seemed happy.

Oronesus glanced up to the sky past the glass roof. "It seems the Herald has arrived."

Ertide leaned back in his chair and sipped at a glass of wine. It was both spicy and sweet, and not nearly strong enough to let him deal with the Rider. "I wonder what possible reason Mathanial could have for arriving unannounced?"

Oronesus frowned at his tone but said nothing. She never sat. They met daily, often spending all day in meetings just like this, and yet she was always on her feet, her many tomes floating around her, just waiting for her summons to reveal the knowledge they contained.

Somewhere distant, the arboretum door burst open with another peal of thunder. Ertide noticed Polapen wince at the sound.

"Where are you?" Mathanial shouted so loudly a couple of birds squeaked in alarm and took flight, flitting through the trees to safety. "Damnit, sister! What are we even doing in this overgrown plant pot?"

Oronesus waited calmly and silently, a patient half smile on her lips. Ertide sipped at his wine and scratched a nail down the side of the chalice making it squeal.

"Which way is... This place is a maze." Mathanial, the Rider, leapt into the air, his pearly wings beating hard as he climbed towards the glass ceiling, the trees below shook from his passing. "Ahh, there you are."

The angel swept down with another beat of his wings and landed in the orchard square, another peal of thunder shaking the entire arboretum the moment his feet touched the ground.

He was a pretty man, was the Rider. Smooth skin the colour of onyx, high cheekbones and piercing grey eyes. He wore leather suitable for riding, faded and stained and well worn. His wings were white as snow, but gold veins snaked their way through the feathers.

The Rider gave his wings a final flap, stirring up dust into eddies that swirled around Ertide's leg and deposited dust in his wine. Then the angel couched his wings and strode forward into the centre of the square, commanding the area with ease. He had such a presence about him, it was as though he filled the space.

"What are we doing here, sister?" Mathanial said, his voice deep and sonorous.

Oronesus folded her arms. "The king wished to spend some time around the trees."

"Did he?" Mathanial asked. "Connecting with nature, are we, Ertide?"

He mocks me in my own palace.

"I merely wished for a change in scenery," Ertide said. "We are not all lucky enough to spend each day gallivanting."

Mathanial roared out a laugh. "Forgive me, Ertide, I meant no disrespect. One day I'll have to take you up on one of my pegasi, hmmm? Show you the wonder of the sky. Then, maybe you'll see why I'm so fond of my gallivanting."

"I would like that. Perhaps seeing the world as you do would broaden my perspective." In truth, he would have loved to ride on the back of a pegasus, but he knew it would never happen, regardless of the Rider's promises. The angels guarded their winged horses far too jealously. No one, not even the king, was allowed to mount one of the beasts without permission from God himself.

"You, boy." Mathanial clicked his fingers at Arandon. "Fetch me a glass of that wine your grandfather is drinking. It smells delicious."

Arandon's eyes boggled, but Ertide gave him a nod and he grumbled, placed his notes on the chair and stomped off in search of more wine. Mathanial watched him go, grinning.

"Does them good to learn a bit of humility," the angel said.

"To what do we owe the pleasure of your visit, Herald?" Ertide asked.

"Pleasure?" Mathanial laughed. "That's a good one, Ertide." The smile slipped from his handsome face. "Why aren't my ships built yet?"

"They take time to build, Herald."

The angel took a step closer and another peal of thunder rumbled as if responding to his anger. "Build them faster."

Ertide made a careless gesture with his goblet, spilling a few drops of wine on the ground. He hoped it would give the impression he was drunk. "Perhaps you should have been more careful with the last ones and not lost them."

"The seas are dangerous, unpredictable."

"Mmm. And what of the expeditions you sent over the Jagger-mounts to the east? I suppose the mountains are also dangerous and unpredictable."

The Rider stared down at Ertide, clenched his fists, lightning crawling around his fingers like electric worms. "You would do well to remember that angel lives were lost on those expeditions as well as human. We have all suffered the dangers of this world together. And our losses were felt more keenly. There are fewer of us, and we live forever."

"Then perhaps we would do well to pull back, spend time consolidating. Gather our resources."

Mathanial laughed sharply. "This is the Age of Exploration, Ertide. Not the Age of... of... Sitting on arses doing nothing."

"All I'm saying, Herald, is..."

"As is God's will," the Rider shouted over him, shutting down the argument.

Ertide stared up into the Rider's dark gaze. He held out for as long as he could, but even his defiance could only go so far. "As is God's will," he muttered.

Arandon returned with a servant in tow carrying a tray with a new pitcher of wine and goblets. Mathanial turned in a swish of wings and snatched one of the goblets, downing the wine in one swallow, then casually tossing the goblet over his shoulder. He was such a careless fop of an angel, headless of anything or anyone he damaged along the way. So intent on his exploration of the world he would destroy the foundations that supported him.

And yet I must bow and scrape to him as with all his kin.

The Rider narrowed his eyes. "There are lands beyond the Sant Dien Empire, Ertide. Beyond Aelegar and the Ice Isles. Beyond the Tvean Sea and the Jaggermounts." He turned and flung out a hand, pointing at Ertide. "I must see it, the world beyond these constricting borders."

"You have wings. Fly yourself there and leave us free of you."

"Ertide," the warning came from Oronesus, glowering, her glow turned fierce.

They have disagreements, yet they are always united against me. Ertide had seen angels argue before, but always to humanity they presented a united front. *As is God's will.*

"If only it were so simple," Mathanial said. "But there are dangers greater than sea or foul weather out there. Too dangerous for one or even a few to go alone. No, we must mount a true expedition. Not the paltry handful we have sent before, not hundreds. Thousands." He pranced around as he spoke, careless of how his words would so quickly become manifest. Of how Ertide would be forced to make it so.

"A grand expedition to new lands," the Rider paced and gesticulated as if speaking to a rapt audience. "No, not new lands. To the old world. Ships larger than any built before. A fleet. Tens of thousands strong. Those with courage and curiosity in their hearts will join me. We will explore. We will conquer. We will tame. All in God's will and his name. Spreading his faith and love and welcome to the dark places of the world."

The Rider spun about, grinning madly, his foolish speech fading to silence. There was an infectious energy to Mathanial. Even now, Ertide could see how he was affecting the others. The servants stared at him with wonder, their tasks forgotten. Even Arandon stood enrapt, an eager smile on his face. If the Rider asked for it then, Ertide's bookish grandson would be the first to sign up to this new grand expedition. It was so easy to get caught up in Mathanial's energy. Ertide knew that first hand, but he'd been listening to the Herald's speeches for over thirty years now and much of their glamour had worn away like colours fading from a once vibrant tapestry.

Ertide cleared his throat and it almost turned into another bloody coughing fit. He had to swallow it down, tapping a hand against his chest. When he finally had control of himself, he found Oronesus watching him with narrowed eyes.

"We do not have the funds," Ertide said.

The Rider threw up his hands, passion quickly replaced with anger again. "The funds. The funds. All you ever talk about, Ertide, is money. Are you truly so obsessed with a few shiny coins? There will be riches for the taking in the old world, Ertide, just waiting for you to reach out and grasp, if that is what your heart so desires."

Ertide sighed. "I cannot build boats from nothing. There are costs involved, Herald. The lumber must be cut, worked. The shipwrights need time and pay to construct the ships." *It's like explaining to a child.*

"Again with the wages. As if coin is more important than the meaning of the age. They are citizens of the Sant Dien Empire, you are their king. Order them to work. Order more of them to work. Anyone not working on my boats should be reassigned immediately."

"And how would we feed them while they work? How would we gather the supplies we will need to keep the expedition alive while it sails?"

"Order others to work the fields."

Ertide pinched the bridge of his nose. He was getting a headache.

"Mathanial..." Oronesus started.

The Rider turned on her, all but snarling. "Quiet, sister. Our father has placed me in charge of this age and I will see his will done. Stick to your dusty books. You are a Fourth Age, a child."

Oronesus closed her mouth and took a step back, seceding the ground. An angel she might be, a child of the God, but she had no real authority here, not when the Herald of the current age was in command.

"Your ships will be built, Herald," Ertide said slowly, feeling exhausted. "Your expedition will be mounted. I will see God's will done. But it cannot be done quickly. I need time."

"Time?" The Rider turned a mocking smile on Ertide. "Have you looked at yourself recently, Ertide? Time is not a resource you have a lot of."

Ertide shot to his feet so fast his head swam, but he blinked away the fuzzy vision. "I am still king, Mathanial, and this is my empire."

The Rider took a thunderous step towards him. "And you think that crown and throne are important? I am the Herald of the Fourth Age. I am chosen by God to see his will carried out, tasked with the making of this age.

"What happened to the fearless Crimson Prince who rode beside me into the fray? Who stood toe to toe with the barbarian horde and shouted *You shall not take my lands*? What happened to your fire, Ertide, the blaze that ran through your veins as surely as it did your ancestors?"

"I made peace, Herald. Peace with Aelegar, peace with the Ice Walkers. I made peace with myself. I got old, and there is no one left to fight."

"But there could be. Stop resisting me, and join me, Ertide. We will battle the wilderness, make war on the unknown. Together. You can be the Crimson Prince again, one last time, riding beside me as we strike out into the darkness and burn away the mists that cover our maps. We will make the unknown known. Forge a new world out of the old. Side by side, as we were always meant to be."

Ertide couldn't help the swell within his chest. Mathanial's words reached him, tugged on that buried part of him that still wanted adventure; the young, brash prince standing on a field of slain enemies, covered in blood, screaming at the retreating horde as they scrambled away from his blade, the Rider beside him wreathed in lightning, blade raised to the sky to summon his pegasi and give chase.

But no. Those days were long gone. That foolish prince was dead and buried, his lust for battle a flame that had been quenched in the blood of so many. He was king now, not prince, and he had an empire to think about, people to protect.

"I see," the Rider said with obvious disdain. He must have seen the decision on Ertide's face. "I thought you would be the one to stand by my side as we brought a united man and angelkind into a new era of exploration. A bold king willing to do what is necessary. I see now how wrong I was."

His voice softened. "You have grown timid, Ertide. Infirmary has made you weak of flesh and doddering of mind. It is so often the way with the fragility of your kind. Mortality breeds such failings." He placed his hands on Ertide's shoulders and pressed down gently. Despite that almost tender touch, his strength was irresistible. Ertide sagged back into his chair before the Rider injured him.

"It is time, Ertide. Time for you to abdicate in favour of a more bold ruler with the courage and discipline to join me in my task. Someone with principles. With joy and passion still flowing through their veins, instead of dust and caution." He glanced at Arandon, grimaced. "Someone else."

It was a step too far. "You do not get to decide when I abdicate, angel!" Ertide spat.

The Rider grinned down at him, arms folded across his chest. Lightning briefly flashed overhead again, brightening the sky. As it faded, Ertide realised the sky was darkening quickly as the sun fled over the western horizon.

"It's almost time for evening prayers, Ertide," the Rider said as he turned and sauntered away. "Make sure to prepare a suitable sacrifice today. You'll need my father's favour in the weeks to come." He laughed and waved over his shoulder. "And build my damned boats."

CHAPTER 4

Bells were ringing all over the city, the call to evening prayer blurted out from every temple, church, shrine, and cathedral. All over Celesgarde, all over every city, town, and village in the Sant Dien Empire, people, Ertide's people, would be laying down their tools, turning their faces to the north, towards Heaven's Light, kneeling and giving prayer.

Praise and worship to an absent God. He almost gave the thought voice, but he couldn't. Even here, alone in his quarters, was he truly alone? *Of course, I'm not, old fool of a man. Jertis is here.*

There was a soft knock at the door, and Ertide looked up from his scout reports. The barbarians of Aelegar were on the move again, claiming peace but roving the southern mountains as though posturing for war. He'd slumped onto the couch as soon as he entered his quarters, put up his weary feet, and let Jertis pull off his boots. Now he was only one blink from dozing away the rest of the evening.

"Sire?" Jertis asked. Ertide sighed and gave him a nod.

Ylnaea glided through on slippered feet as soon as the door was open. "God's Favour, husband," she said cheerily.

The bells were giving Ertide a headache. "And to you, wife," he said more sourly than he intended.

She was a beautiful woman, was Ylnaea. A healthy plumpness to her cheeks and figure, pale skin with rosy cheeks, hair as red as a forge, and a fascinating scatter of freckles all across her nose and right cheek. She was also so damnably young. Ertide had grandchildren almost twice her age. But the angels had decided she was to be his new wife.

God's will done once more.

"You can leave now, Jertis," Ylnaea said softly. "I will attend my husband."

Jertis glanced over at Ertide. Ertide rolled his eyes, then nodded quickly before his wife could take offence. In short order, Jertis was ushered out, and the door was closed behind him. Ylnaea whisked into the room like a spring breeze, disturbing everything and making chaos out of order. She pushed away his notes and reports, without a care for how they were stacked. His half drunk glass of wine was taken away, the contents thrown hissing into the hearth. She pushed at his legs until he was sitting on the couch instead of lounging. Within mere moments, any thought of relaxation was vanished and the tide of drowsiness that had been tugging at Ertide retreated to leave a bare and rocky consciousness.

"Do you hear the bells?" Ylnaea prodded meaningfully.

Ertide nodded. "They are a little hard to miss."

"Then it is time for evening prayers, husband. Time to give thanks for the day, for the God's Favour, for the life and protection he provides."

"Yes," Ertide agreed slowly. "All that good stuff."

Ylnaea's face grew stony and cold, her rosy cheeks no longer seeming a healthy glow, but a painted facade. "You missed the morning prayers, husband."

"I rather consider that your fault, wife." He smiled in an attempt to brook peace. Ylnaea did not smile back.

There can be no peace. No compromise here. Only servitude. That's why they chose her for me. A beautiful, pious whip to crack over my back.

She held out her hands and he took them. So soft, but with a strength like iron beneath. She helped pull him to his feet and together they sank down onto the prayer mat before the hearth. The damned bells were still ringing and Ertide wished they'd stop long enough to let him think.

"Have you prepared a sacrifice, husband?" Ylnaea asked. "Something special to make up for missing morning prayers."

"Of course I have," Ertide lied.

Sacrifice, the Fourth Tennant. A daily ritual of giving to the God. Something important, a thing you wanted or needed. No worship was more divine than giving away something you couldn't do without.

He reached over to the table and scattered his notes about until he found what he was looking for. A scrap of paper with some coloured squiggles on it. A red circle with some wavy lines below it that he was assured was meant to be him. A black squiggle on top for his crown. And then a yellow scribble below that was apparently a dog. Murtan, his youngest grandson had drawn it and handed it to him just that evening, grinning wide as only a child can. Apparently the dog was a hopeful little addition because his parents wouldn't let him have a puppy, so he was asking the king instead.

"Hmm," Ylnaea said sourly.

Ertide looked down at the little drawing. He didn't want to give it up, to see it burn. It was a gift from Murtan, the little boy who was all pudgy smiles and talked so fast his words ran together until even his own parents couldn't understand him. It was his grandson's eager wish for a puppy. He didn't want to give it up, but that was the point of sacrifice. Giving to the God that which you treasured most to prove your love and devotion to him above all else.

As the bells continued their cacophony blaring out all over the empire, Ylnaea led them through prayers.

"Bless us, God, for all we do we do in your name and with your grace. The food on our plates, the love in our hearts, the blood in our veins, all is by your will. Protect us against the terrors of the dark and of the past, from those who would wish us harm. We thank you for all that you have given us. Our lives, our prosperity, our freedom, our protectors and guides your children."

Ertide blocked it all out. Ylnaea's prayer, the racket of the bells, the clamouring of his own voice reciting along with her. He stared down at the little picture and instead offered his own little promise to his grandson.

You'll get your puppy, Murtan. I promise you.

"Your sacrifice, husband," Ylnaea prompted, her prayer finally finished.

Ertide scrunched up the little drawing and threw it angrily into the flames. His wife did not seem to notice his frustration. He screwed his eyes shut and blocked out Ylnaea's words as she completed the daily prayer.

It was all just too much. Everything they had was only theirs as long as God's will allowed it. Everything they did was to serve him or his angels, to further the goal of the age. The Rider would beggar the empire in his quest for exploration and Ertide would have to facilitate it. The angels would choose his heir, force him to abdicate his throne, and he could do nothing but smile and pretend it was all for the best.

He was king in name only. Powerless. His path dictated by the light that shone from Heaven. He could not even resist. To so much as speak against God's will, even in private, would see his crown torn from his head for blasphemy.

Is this why you gave in to their every whim and demand, father? A puppet on the throne because you had no other choice? How can I hope to resist when God sees everything but my own thoughts? How can anyone resist?

And yet, what of crime? What of the criminals that even now stole from honest folk down in the city? God did not send his angels to them to bring them to justice. What of the barbarians in Aelegar? They were forever raiding the empire, making war then vanishing back into their mountain strongholds that even the angels said they could not find. Did the God not see them? Why were the Rider's expeditions so important, his desire to explore the old world so vital if God watched from Heaven and saw all? Surely he already knew all that was out there?

Is it possible he does not see all? I cough up blood daily, and yet no angel has asked after my health. Ertide wondered how much he was willing to risk? Would he be able to wager his own life, and anyone he spoke to, over the chance that God was not omnipresent?

"Husband?"

Ertide opened his eyes, blinking away blurry vision. Ylnaea stood before him, her dress in a heap at her feet, her skin naked and soft, glowing by the light of the fire.

"Oh," Ertide said. "Are we... Ylnaea, I..."

Stop stammering like a young boy never seen a pair of tits before. He was king and an old man, it was time to start acting like it.

"Ylnaea, perhaps we could take a night off? I do not have the stamina I used..."

"Nonsense, husband." Ylnaea knelt before him, her nimble fingers quickly undoing the lace of his shirt. "God's second tenant is prosperity. There is no greater form of prosperity than bearing a child."

"I'm an old man."

"You are my husband," Ylnaea said so earnestly. "And you are the king. This is your duty." She finished undoing his lace and pulled his shirt over his head, then stood and walked towards the bedroom. She stopped at the door and turned back to him, her eyes so intense he felt the need to look away. "As is God's will."

Ertide ground his teeth. He hated those four words more than anything. The finality of them, the futility of arguing against them. The sheer arrogance contained in four short words.

Ertide stood slowly, his knees popping from the effort, and he let Ylnaea lead him into the bedroom, but he could not hide the bitterness from his voice. "As is God's will."

CHAPTER 5

Something light and airy tickled Ertide's nose and he sneezed himself awake.

"Morning, handsome," said a man's voice.

Ertide blinked away morning haze to find feathers dark as night draped over him. He startled and shuffled away, aiming for the edge of his bed.

"Leaving so soon?" the angel said, chuckling.

Ertide recognised the voice then, and he stopped, sighed, and pushed back the wing. "Moon, you puckered cat arse. What are you doing in my bed? Am I still in my bed?"

It was a struggle to focus on his surroundings, but there was his wardrobe, his washbasin, the grand painting of Saint Dien leading her Exemplars to battle hanging above a cold hearth.

"It looked comfortable," Moon said, a teasing note in his voice. "And you were so peaceful, all wrinkly and snoring, just like a babe not a day free from his mother's purse."

Moon was a slight man, shorter than Ertide by a good head. He was shorter than all the other angels. His skin was pale as milk, his hair dark as coal and his wings darker still. He was also mad as a bag full of crickets, and Ertide loved him for it.

"What happened to Ylnaea?" Ertide asked as he blearily sat up and gathered the sheets around him.

"Who?" Moon asked innocently.

"My wife."

Moon guffawed. "What? No, Ertide, you're married to Giliana."

Ertide sighed and stared at the angel sharing his bed.

"Oh shit," Moon said, his smile dropping. "How long was I gone this time?"

Ertide considered it. Last time he'd seen his friend it had been a Winter's Eve. Giliana had still been alive so before the plague of Ice Lung swept through the capital.

"Five years, I think?" Ertide said.

Moon brightened and clicked his fingers. "Winter's Eve!"

"Three months after the peace treaty with Aelegar was signed."

"I remember!" Moon grinned as if seeing the sunrise for the first time. "How much did we have to drink?"

"A lot."

"Emrik fell asleep in that maid's cleavage. She looked fit to slap him back to the Third Age."

Ertide chuckled as he remembered. "She did. He apparently liked it. He married Tresalla halfway through that winter. They have a son now, Conran. Though she was never a maid, Moon."

"Really? She kept bringing us drinks."

Ertide clapped his friend on the shoulder. "You kept threatening to read her if she didn't."

"Oh crap. I didn't, did I? That's not why I left?"

"Not as far as I know. Come the morning, you were just gone again. Where did you go, Moon?"

The angel sprang from the bed and stretched out his wings. "Same place I always go, I think. I..." He looked lost for a moment, then sighed heavily. "But I'm back. And we need to catch up. Tell me everything. You have a new wife? What happened to Giliana?"

Ertide sighed. "Ice Lung." He shook his head when he saw Moon was about to ask how bad it was.

"Oh. I'm sorry, old friend. I liked her."

Ertide nodded sadly. He missed Giliana every day. "She hated you."

Moon grinned. "Impossible. Now get up, old man. Let's catch up properly over breakfast. It's been... years since I last ate, I think."

Ertide would be lying if he said he didn't envy Moon's eternal youth just a little, but just being around the angel leant him new energy and he felt younger than he had in years. Jertis tsked when he opened the door to the king's quarters and saw Moon lounging on the dining table, kicking his legs back and forth. The servant ordered breakfast brought inside and went about with his daily cleaning up, pointedly ignoring the angel, except to shoo him out of the way occasionally.

They chatted as they ate, catching up on all that had happened. Ertide slathered butter on a pasty and bit into it, spilling crumbs everywhere. It was almost as if the angel had never left, they fell back into their old friendship so easily. Ertide had known Moon his entire life, from child to man to king to the dusty old relic he was now. He shared more history with the angel than with anyone, even his own children. There was a comfort in that familiarity.

But why has he returned now of all times?

Ertide didn't like the thought, but he couldn't deny it. Now, when his faith was waning lowest, when he entertained so many thoughts of heresy and rebellion. The Herald of the Fourth Age had just a day ago threatened to force Ertide into abdication, and then suddenly Moon reappears after five years of absence. Was it the angel's seer sight, warning him of things to come, that he would be needed again? Or was it God sending his most trusted emissary, his Apostle, to keep a warier eye on a straying old king?

He had no way to know the truth of it, and there was nothing he could do even should he know the truth, so Ertide decided he would spend time with his old friend while time they had.

"Do you remember the time you distracted Orphus?" Moon asked after they were done with breakfast and Ertide was getting ready to address the day. The morning prayer bells would start ringing soon enough.

"Just about," Ertide said. "That was... I was eight or nine?"

"Was it truly so long ago?" Moon asked. "Seems like yesterday. What was it you asked him?"

Ertide paused with his hand on the door, desperately trying to drudge up the memory. Jertis hovered nearby, uncomfortable and Ertide suddenly realised it had been years since he'd last opened a door himself.

"I asked him to explain the finer points of the offhand parry cut he was so fond of at the time," Ertide said eventually, the memory flooding back like a lake with its dam burst. "You crept up behind him and painted his greaves with honey."

Moon bellowed out a laugh. "He had stray dogs following him around for days, licking at his ankles. He had no idea why."

Ertide chuckled. "That was all your idea. I could have got in so much trouble." His chuckle almost turned into a cough and he had to swallow it, bending over and feigning being overcome with laughter.

"Pah!" Moon said. "You were the king in waiting already. What trouble could you have gotten in?"

Ertide sobered a little at that. *What trouble, indeed? Does the God overlook his favourite son's pranks on purpose?*

He pulled open the door to find a cadre of servants waiting for him on the other side. No doubt they wished to clean away the breakfast plates before morning prayers. Arandon was already there waiting, sat in his plush chair, note board on his lap.

"Heaven's Light, Grandfa..." Arandon faltered when he saw Moon. He cleared his throat. "Grandfather." He scowled at Moon. "Apostle."

"Oh!" Moon sounded like he'd just stepped in dog shit. "I'd actually forgotten about that title. Please call me Moon. Or uncle Moon."

Arandon sighed. "No."

"That's a shame. You know, I was there when you were born, red faced and squealing like a piglet. I held you in my arms, dangled a feather in front of your face."

Arandon stood sharply, the chair legs grinding across the floor. "Is there a point to this story, Apostle?"

Moon shook his head breezily. "None at all."

"Wonderful. Grandfather, the plans for the Grand Samir courtyard have been sent to your study, awaiting your decision. The delegation from the Ice Isles is here to see you. Again. There are..."

"Anything important?" Ertide asked as he started strolling down the corridor, leaving the others to catch up. Moon skipped at his side and took his arm, threading his own through it.

"It's all important, Grandfather."

"Anything urgent, Arandon?" Ertide asked. "Moon has been gone for so long. I thought I'd take a day and show him how the family are growing."

Moon gasped excitedly. "That would be wonderful. Why, last time I saw you, little Arandon, you were still gulping down milk from your nanny's wrinkled teats."

One of the trailing servants sniggered.

Arandon bristled. "I was not." He smoothed down his robe with one hand.

"No? Quite right, you were far too old. Perhaps you were just trying to court the old cow instead."

"I will reschedule all your meetings until tomorrow, Grandfather. Morning bells are in five minutes." With that, Arandon sketched off a short bow, and turned, striding away down a different corridor.

"Well," Moon said. "He certainly inherited Rikkan's sense of humour. How someone so grouchy ever dribbled from your loins, I'll never know."

Ertide stopped in front of his private shrine and waited for Jertis to open the door. "You shouldn't needle him so, Moon. Arandon is a serious lad, but he's also meticulous and driven, with a head for negotiation."

"Oh yes, he sounds like a riot." The first of the bells out in the city started ringing, quickly joined by more and more. Moon skipped through into the king's shrine ahead of Ertide, much to the obvious annoyance of Jertis. "Besides, old friend, it's my role to needle. I was put upon this world to poke and prod and make people uncomfortable and want to scream." He turned and raised an eyebrow. "Everyone but you, apparently. For some reason I can't seem to drive you away."

"It's alright, Jertis," Ertide said.

The man looked uncomfortable. "No one but the king is allowed in the king's shrine, sire."

Ertide smiled. "Thank you for explaining that to me."

Jertis paled.

"Go," Ertide said, waving at the man. "Attend to your own prayers. If

Moon starts making too much trouble, I'll just throw him out the window."

"What a threat," Moon drawled. "If only I could fly."

Ertide closed the door to the shrine and turned the key in the lock. Jertis would hurry away to join the other servants in the palace chapel, listening to one angel or another read a sermon from the Rite of the Divine. Everyone, be they king or queen, servant or soldier, street rat or merchant gathered to the churches and temples for the morning bells to face the north and pray towards Heaven's Light, to listen to the God's words spoken through his children.

A chill breeze gusted into the shrine as Moon threw open the window. Dust stirred on the floor, and Ertide frowned at the mess in the small chamber. No one but the king was allowed to step foot in the king's shrine, and that meant he was responsible for keeping the place clean and tidy. In his younger years, just after his father's death and his coronation, Ertide came here daily, prayed on his knees, read from the book. And after the morning bells had died away, he'd spend some time sweeping, cleaning, even polishing the sconces and replacing candles. It had been pleasant to ground himself in menial tasks. But he'd long since fallen out of the practice. There was just too much to do these days, too many people clawing for his attention. It had been months at least since he'd even stepped into the room.

The shrine was a mess. Coated in dust. Spider webs hung in the corners and he smelled the musty scent of mouse droppings. The sconces were rusting, the candles long since burned out and never replaced. A tapestry on the wall, depicting the Archangel and the Saint in glorious battle against a demon, was a faded rag, fraying at the edges and in need of a good beating to work out the dust.

"This place has seen better days," Moon said. He wiped a hand across the sill, shooing away a recalcitrant spider, then leapt up to sit on the sill, resting his back against the window frame. He stretched a wing out over the drop and sighed in pleasure. A cool breeze ruffled his feathers.

Ertide paced slowly through the shrine. There was a single wooden pew, a dusty old tome sitting upon it; The Rite of the Divine. "This was my father's personal copy," Ertide said. "It never left this room. He made notes in the margins, studied it intensely every day." He hefted the book from the bench and blew the dust from the faded, worn cover. "When he died... when I was crowned, I found a note in here, laid on top of the book, addressed to me. What did it say? It's been so long." He struggled to remember the words.

"*This belongs to you now, son. Care for it well, as I have tried.*"

"Hmmm," Moon said airily, dangling one leg over the side of the sill. "Remarkably brief for Terin. Your father never met a word that didn't need to drag a few friends along for company."

Ertide smiled briefly. It was not the full message.

Ertide,

This belongs to you now, son. Care for it well, as I have tried. The truth in these pages, behind the ink and beyond the words, is the truth of our empire. It is bloody. It is broken. And it is not what you think.

We are a people built on lies and ruled by fear. I have tried to uncover what I could, but so much has been lost, and the seeking of it is more dangerous than you know.

It is unfair, this task I leave to you. I recognise now, I was not strong enough to shoulder the burden, nor to shuck the chains, so I threw you into the fire, hoping to forge in my son a better image of myself, one who is not so weak and so scared.

Destroy this note, son, and let no other see it. Hide the book, it is never to leave this room for the notes within are heresy. I do not know how much his eyes see, but I know my thoughts are safe. I only hope these words are, too.

Be stronger than me. Rule well and find our freedom. Hold to your family above all else for there is power in blood.

In love,
Your father

It was that note which had started Ertide questioning his faith. He had been as pious as Ylnaea before that, but there was something in his father's last words that made him look differently upon the book the note was sitting on. Ertide had combed through that book, staring at the notes in the margins, studying the odd pages that had been torn free. Yet he could make no sense of it. Eventually he had given up trying. His father had wanted him to grasp something he simply could not. He was a warrior and a general, not a scholar.

Ertide placed the book back on the pew and leaned against the sill, looking out over his city. The crowded buildings, the cobbled streets, the churches with their bells making such a racket. The people flowing about, searching for a place to pray. And towering over it all, the God-made mountain of the Overlook. If he peered up at the top of the mountain, he could just about make out the Shrine of Ages. He still remembered the sound of the bell that the shrine protected as it rung out four times to signal the beginning of the Fourth Age. It made every other bell in the world seem a quiet, paltry thing.

To the North, far beyond the limits of Celesgarde, beyond the horizon even, only just visible in the morning light, a bright beam of light shone down from the sky. Many leagues away, that light blazed upon Heaven's Gate, whether night or day or stormiest weather, that light always shone upon the gate.

"You're brooding," Moon said, a wry smile tugging at his lips. A dark wing buffeted Ertide in the face.

Ertide shrugged. "I do that these days. A benefit of age, I get to be grumpy and no one asks why."

"When did you get so old?" Moon asked, his face a picture of innocence.

"I was old before your last disappearance."

"Were you? Noooo. You were wrinkled, sure. But not old."

Ertide laughed. "It sneaks up on you."

"I wouldn't know." Moon kicked his feet over the drop some more. "I never get to be old. What is it that bloody book calls me?"

"The Forever Child."

"Ah! All I do is try to bring joy and levity to the world, and they lump me with such a belittling name."

"It's in the book, so they're your father's words."

Moon grinned like a frog with a fly. "Are they?"

The bells started falling silent all over the city. Gathering was over and now it was time to pray. Ertide shuffled back a few steps, brushed some of the dust from the mat, and knelt upon it. The window opened north, staring directly towards Heaven's Light.

"What are you doing?" Moon asked innocently.

"Praying."

"Oh." He leaned back and whistled a brisk tune as he dangled his leg and stared out the window.

Ertide closed his eyes. He never led prayers anymore, preferring to let others do the talking while he considered other things.

"What are you praying for?"

"I... I don't know." Prayers were all about giving thanks to the God for everything he provided humanity. For freeing them from the demons, for his continued protection. For the children, his angels, that shepherded humanity to prosperity and glory. Only Ertide wasn't grateful for the angels. Mostly he just wished they'd bugger off and let him rule his empire. Except Moon.

"I guess I'll pray because I'm grateful for you."

"Ahhh," Moon's face crumpled as though holding back tears, then he grinned wide and laughed. "You are such a melodramatic fop sometimes, Ertide."

Ertide had to concede that point. "What do you pray for, Moon?"

"Me?" Moon laid a hand against his chest. "Nothing. What would be the point?"

"I thought all you angels prayed. To give thanks to your father for creating you and gifting you with his divine strength."

Moon stared at Ertide incredulously. "Would you like to hear a secret, old friend?" the angel asked in a hushed voice.

"Now who's being melodramatic?"

"Oh you want drama?" Moon sat up and leapt nimbly to his feet, balancing on the sill. He stared at Ertide with wide eyes as blue as the sky. "Here's a secret, one of many, never to be told." He leaned forward, clinging to the sill. "God can't hear you."

With that, Moon shot to his feet and leapt backwards out into the drop.

Ertide struggled to his feet, his knees popping, his back groaning in aching agony. He reached the sill just in time to see Moon spread his dark wings and glide away, a braying laugh bursting from his lips and echoing around the palace grounds.

CHAPTER 6

Ertide threw open the shrine door and limped out on aching legs. The sudden movement was making him lightheaded, spots dancing around his eyes. He had let himself go, blaming age for inevitable deterioration, but in truth it was disuse that was making him so weak. It had been many years since he had trained with his sword, even longer since he had moved at anything faster than a brisk walk. Now, though, now he ran.

His footsteps rang on the stone floor, echoing down empty corridors. No family, no servants, no soldiers. The palace felt empty. It was a lie, of course. The palace was not empty, but everyone was crowding into the chapels. For the next thirty minutes, almost every person in his empire was clamouring to hear the words of God's children.

Ertide rushed down the steps of the great staircase far faster than was safe, one hand barely trailing the banister. He hit the bottom out of breath, and staggered to a halt, panting and coughing into his hand. When he was done, there was bright red blood in his hand. He stared at it for a moment, feeling the icy talons clutching his chest. Then he wiped the blood on his britches and forged on. He had no time to waste, he had to find Moon before his empire woke from its enforced sermons.

He chose a side corridor that led to the servants' entrance. Even now, during morning prayers, there would be soldiers on the main gate. They would not stop him, not daring to accost the king, but they would follow him, and he didn't want that. He needed to speak to Moon alone. Better to slip out via the servants' entrance.

The corridor ahead was blocked with people, three bodies deep, pressed around a doorway. Light and warmth and the sound of an angelic voice spilled from within. Too many people and not enough angels to give the morning prayers. All over the empire it would be like this; people, his people, clinging to balconies, squashing against doors, peering in through windows, to see God's children, to hear them as they dished out his words.

His lies, if my father is to be believed. The book played on Ertide's mind, the notes his father had made that he had never been able to decipher.

Ertide started squeezing into the press of bodies. There were some grumbles, a few nudged elbows, but no one even turned to see who was pushing through behind the crowd, so intent they were on the angel. Ertide recognised the sermon, one from the poet, Rook.

It was the story of the Shadow Knight, one of the Knights Exemplar who fought with Saint Dien against the demons. It was a tale of loss and a decade long quest to take back what was stolen. Ertide had heard it more times than he could count. A demon stole the Shadow Knight's voice and he joined the Saint in the hope of slaying the demon and taking back what was ripped from him. And when finally the Shadow Knight was victorious, his voice under his command once again, still he said nothing, choosing instead to give his voice to God. He sacrificed the thing that was most precious to him, the thing he fought so hard for, to prove his love, his devotion, and his gratitude.

Ertide's father had made notes on the story in his book. A scrawl in the margins that said: *Vows of silence are not uncommon in the temples, but look deeper. Seek the truth. Caro's Legacy: A Saint's Duty. Page 92.*

Ertide had never even heard of Caro's Legacy: A Saint's Duty, and when he scoured the palace library for a copy, there was no indication the book even existed.

"Sire?" whispered the final man in the press as Ertide squeezed past him. He looked to be one of the stable hands, a wiry man with a jutting chin and a mop of blond hair.

Ertide raised a finger to his mouth and winked. A little secret shared between king and servant. It would bind the man to silence far more surely than any order.

"Heaven's Light, sire," the man whispered, smiling.

Ertide turned back, taking the man's hand. "Can I borrow your cloak?"

He stole out the servants' entrance into an empty city, cloaked in a tatty old cloak that stank of horse. It was somewhat liberating to be free of crown and expectation, and his constant train of servants and minders. But it was strange seeing Celesgarde so empty. The cobbled streets were cold and bare. Here and there, a horse stood tethered to a post or a wild dog crossed from one alley to another, but there were no people.

Ertide looked to the sky, but Moon was gone. Long gone now. He wasn't even sure why he had thought he could run out of the palace and catch up with his friend. The angel had wings! He could be halfway to Vael by now. Ertide shook his head.

Or is this what Moon wanted? Did he know you'd follow him? It was impossible to guess. Moon had the seer's sight, able to see past and future as surely as the present. *But if he had known I would follow him, what did he want me to see?*

The first church Ertide came to wasn't just crowded, it was a churning mass of panicked citizens trying to get close, to hear even a word from the angel within. The grand building stood alone in a square, a squat structure with a single towering spire rising up, housing the bell to summon people every morning. People crowded the steps, clung to the brickwork, peered in through windows. They spilled out onto the street, straining against each other, pushing and pulling in vain attempts to get closer. Ertide stared in disgust at the madness.

Children were left unattended at the edges, some crying, others taken to fighting each other. One young girl charged past him, chasing a cat. There was no sign of a parent.

"Such chaos," Ertide mused aloud before clamping down on the words.

"You think this is bad?" Moon said from behind. Ertide spun to find his old friend leaning against a nearby stone wall, a wry smile on his face. "This is close to your palace, Ertide. The people here are your nobles and merchants. The wealthy are still just about clinging to their sense of propriety."

"Moon, what did you..."

Moon held up a slender finger and glanced pointedly to the side. Ertide followed his gaze to find one of the young children had drifted closer and was staring open-mouthed at the angel. Moon went down on one knee in front of the girl and leaned in close. Then he stuck out his tongue and made a wet farting sound. The girl giggled in glee and Moon leapt into the sky, taking flight with three powerful beats of his wings and soaring over the roof tops.

Ertide sighed. "I'm going to kill you when I get hold of you, Moon."

He sent one last glance at the throng surrounding the church, then pulled the hood up over his head and set off after Moon, striding down an alleyway.

He passed empty homes, shops left unattended, carts trundling gently down the streets as the horses still attached milled about looking for food. Every couple of streets, another church or chapel stood, surrounded by too many people all struggling to hear the words spoken within.

Nobody recognised him, most didn't pay him the slightest attention, but those who did often shot him dirty looks as though he might try to push them away and claim their spot. It was almost as though each of them, his citizens, equated proximity to the church as a measure of their own devotion. The words, the meaning of the words, the messages of the angels did not truly matter. The only thing that mattered was being close enough to hear even a snatch of those divine voices, even if you had to step over a fallen neighbour to get close enough.

He passed another square and another church. This one was a tall, grand structure with ornate windows that seemed to glow, as if the light within could not be contained. The people here were poorer, dirtier, but still crowded around the church. What struck Ertide was that the homes around the square were dilapidated. Rotting wood, broken windows, sagging door frames. While the church stood as a pristine beacon, the homes around it were crumbling.

Eventually he realised where Moon was leading him. Saint Dien's Cathedral sat in the heart of Celesgarde, in the shadow of the Overlook. The cathedral was a grand structure climbing above the streets around it, with eight double doors on the longest side and four on the shorter. It sloped upward into an arched roof and had seven towers, each with its own bell. People crowded the cathedral, even thicker than they had the churches and chapels. The crowd was a churning mass, hundreds, maybe even thousands strong. Ertide didn't even try to get close.

Moon stood at the mouth of an alley, staring at the cathedral with dark wings couched and arms crossed. Ertide stood beside his old friend and surveyed the chaos.

"See there," Moon said, nodding. "Humanity at its best."

Ertide saw a young man lying on the cobbles, a red stain spreading around him. He'd been stabbed, and he was dead. No one paid him any attention. No one cared. Not the men and women clamouring for the angel's words, nor the children waiting at the edges of the crowd. Not even the soldiers, the men and women of the First Legion who had also gathered for the morning prayers. A man had been murdered, in sight of the cathedral, during prayers to God, and no one cared.

Ertide remembered another page in his father's book, another note the old king had written in the margins.

When faith becomes religion, and worship is enforced with threat and fear, morality actual suffers in the shadow of morality implied.

And here it was, his father's words given form and clarity of meaning. The God preached kindness for your fellow man, yet the angels offered fear of punishment for defiance. The threat of heresy was stamped down without mercy. And so his people were desperate to be seen to worship, that they missed the principles.

"It was not always this way?" Ertide asked.

Moon shook his head. "It was not."

"What happened?"

"Corruption takes root in even the cleanest waters when there is no current." The angel sounded sad.

The bells started ringing, a few at first, then more and more until the city was a cacophony. The people moved, rippled, drifted away like smoke from a dying fire. Morning prayers were over and they had done their due diligence in worship, now it was time to work. Most people walked around the dead man in the street, not looking, refusing to look. Eventually some of the soldiers took notice and dragged the body away.

"I should head back to the palace before I am missed," Ertide said quietly once the bells had stopped and most of the people were gone.

The city that had so recently felt abandoned, empty save for the churches, now seethed and thronged, alive once again. The streets were busy with people moving too and fro, about their morning business, calling to each other, some cheerily, some not. Shops and workhouses rang with industry. An angel flew overhead so swiftly Ertide could not recognise them.

"You wanted to show me that, Moon," Ertide said as they walked. "Why?"

"It seemed important," Moon said. He frowned. "At the time." The angel was ever that way, ruled by instinct.

"Wait!" Ertide pulled Moon to a stop. They were in the middle of the street, people moving past them on either side. Some stared at the angel and his dark wings, whispering prayers or the like, but just as many ignored them, hoping not to gain the attention of one of God's children. Ertide grabbed Moon's arm and pulled him to the side of the street, just in front of an alley mouth.

"You said he cannot hear me? Back in the king's shrine."

"Did I?" Moon's voice quavered a little.

"Is it true?" Ertide demanded. "Tell me, Moon."

The angel shrugged free of Ertide's grip, easy to do for one with divine strength. "Who knows, Ertide? You know me, I say all sorts of things. I'm the forever child, the fool." He was not smiling, and there was no mirth in his voice. "God's little prank on the world. I am the punchline to a joke no one cared enough to hear."

Ertide took a step forward and Moon backed up a step. "Do not ask, old friend," Moon said. "Some truths cut deeper than any sword. Some wounds cannot be healed. I should go." He turned away and ran a few steps, his wings unfurling.

Ertide reached out to grab his friend, but he felt the familiar tightness in his chest. "Wait..." He clamped a hand over his mouth, trying to swallow the cough, but it was too late. It burst from him into a wracking fit and he felt hot blood in his hand.

When Ertide straightened up past the icy hands in his chest, he found Moon frozen, staring at him with eyes turned dark as midnight.

"Shit!" Ertide cursed and staggered forward, trying to pull the angel out of the street. He'd seen this before, when Moon's visions took hold and he became unstuck in time, his sight roving across the past, present, and future as if all were one. The angel often disappeared for years at a time when such fits of vision took him.

"A thousand years of death," Moon muttered, his head darting like a bird. "The old ones gather, hand over hand over hand. A face of ivory, rattling bones. She brings chaos to order. A stagnant dynasty clinging to the new world. What is dead cannot be reborn. The sky bleeds when the light dies. Day after day after day, it bleeds. Unburnt and unburdened, new saints to break the old. The son must kill the father. When the bloodlines mix a weakness is born. She comes to set me free. You're dying." He gasped and his vision cleared, the darkness draining from his eyes and his gaze locked with Ertide's. Moon smiled. "I can save him!"

CHAPTER 7

An hour after the morning prayers ended, Ertide and Moon strolled back onto the palace grounds. The soldiers at the gates looked a little alarmed to have missed their king slipping out, but they didn't get to dictate where and when he moved about in his own kingdom. Jertis was beside himself, and half the palace in an uproar looking for their missing king. Arandon was with him.

"Grandfather, you can't just run off like that!" Arandon said, fretting over Ertide as though he were a child.

"Can't I?" Ertide said dangerously as he mounted the steps up to the palace. He paused before entering. He desperately wanted to sit down and have a glass of wine, but there were more important things to do. "Where's your father?"

"Rikkan?" Arandon said. He shrugged, a sulky look on his face. None of Rikkan's children liked their father much. "Where else? In the sparring yard."

Ertide glanced at Moon. The angel shrugged.

"God isn't watching," Moon had said after his fit of visions. "But he can look through the eyes of his angels. Only one at a time, he cannot be everywhere all at once, but he can choose to look through any of his children's eyes at any time. The angel will know their vision is being shared, their ears and other senses, too, but they cannot refuse it.

"Even you?" Ertide had asked. "Aren't you worried telling me this?"

Moon had laughed. "Oh, not me. I am... different. Unique. Imperfect. But yes, I'm worried. He may not be able to hear us through me, but others can listen in and tell any angel they find. He has eyes and ears everywhere, old friend, so I implore you, only tell who you can trust. Really trust. You have to be certain or else... God is not merciful."

Ertide thought about it now. He'd been thinking about it the whole way back to the palace. He trusted Rikkan. His oldest son was a brute at times, only ever interested in combat, but he was also not particularly pious. He skipped morning prayers as often as Ertide, and the notes he sent often bordered on heretical. If there was one person Ertide could trust, it was Rikkan. It had to be.

It takes more than one person to birth a conspiracy.

Ertide hurried down the steps and started towards the sparring yards instead. Jertis rushed after him and Ertide pulled the ratty cloak from his shoulders and dumped it in the man's arms.

"Where did you go, Grandfather?" Arandon called.

"To see my city," Ertide called over his shoulder.

"Why?"

Ertide didn't bother answering. He knew Arandon wouldn't follow him. The lengths he'd go to avoid his father knew no bounds.

The clash of steel, the shouts of effort, the smell of leather and metal and sweat. They brought back longings Ertide had thought he had long ago left behind. It had been many years since he'd last been to the sparring grounds, even longer since he'd last fought in them, and longer still since he'd charged into battle alongside the Rider. The Crimson Prince had once been a terror on the battlefield, but no longer. He left the fighting to younger men and women, and these days none were feared so well as Rikkan Hostain, the Mad Dog of the Crown. There was no fight he was not willing to take. And he never lost.

Ertide found his eldest son watching a bout. The sparring grounds were split into a dozen sand and dirt arenas, each with its own wooden benches surrounding. All dozen were in use; soldiers of the First Legion fighting to keep themselves in prime condition mostly. But Rikkan was watching a very different type of match. The twins were facing off against the Archangel himself.

"Father," Rikkan said as Ertide stepped up beside him. "Fool."

Moon chuckled. "Glad to see you remember me, Prince Spear Up His Arse."

Rikkan crossed his arms and said no more. He was a tall man, broad of shoulder, but more rangy than Ertide had been in his youth. He kept his hair short, his beard unkempt, and never said more words than was necessary. Ertide loved his eldest son deeply, but Rikkan was not a man to rule or to lead. He was a flood to be unleashed at the right time to wash away all before him.

"Do they stand a chance?" Ertide asked, waving a hand towards the sparring grounds.

Rikkan scoffed. "None of my children are worth the leather that wraps their hilts. Too much of their mother in them, all of them, mores the pity."

Emrik glanced over from inside the sparring arena, flourishing his sword in a foolish display. "I heard that, father."

Rikkan stared coldly at his eldest son. "Then perhaps you should also heed it. Get on with it, Orphus. Show my children the weakness in their blood."

Orphus, the Archangel was a towering vision of strength. Standing almost twice as tall as any mortal man, he was clad head to toe in shining golden armour so that only his glowing azure eyes were visible. His wings shimmered silver like fire glinting off a polished blade. Ertide had always found the angels of the First Age to be eerily intimidating. They never removed their armour. Even the other angels had no idea what Orphus looked like underneath all that heaven-forged steel.

The Archangel held out a gauntleted hand and a sword fell from the sky like a lightning bolt. The angel caught it just before it struck the floor and settled into a battle ready stance, his azure eyes sparkling in the dark depths of his helm.

"Come then Emrik, Merian. Show me what you have learned." He had such a warm, welcoming voice, like a campfire on a snowy eve. It was almost easy to forget Orphus was the greatest warrior the world had ever seen. Easy to forget how many lives his swords had taken.

"What do you think, brother?" Merian said cheerily as she placed her own helm atop her head and hefted her sword and shield. Both twins wore plate armour to match the angel, and yet he towered over them.

Emrik circled the Archangel, his two hander held ready. "That I'd enjoy this spanking a lot more if it was at the hands of a prettier angel."

Emrik darted forward, drawing the angel's attention, then pulled back. A feint. Merian closed in from behind, shield raised and sword slashing. Orphus shifted his feet only slightly, spun his sword around and stabbed out behind him, under his wings. Merian blocked, but the thrust had enough power it sent her skidding backwards in the sand. Emrik charged and Orphus met him blade to blade. Three ringing blows echoed around the arena, each one punctuated by Emrik's dramatic shout. But he looked like he was moving so slowly compared to the angel. Orphus parried a fourth strike, then struck the pommel of his sword into Emrik's helm, sending him staggering away. The Archangel turned his full attention on Merian.

"They're putting up a decent fight," Ertide mused.

Rikkan scoffed again. "The angel is holding back. If this was a true battle, both of them would be dead a dozen times over by now."

It had ever been a disappointment to Rikkan that none of his children had taken to combat quite like him. The twins were decent enough with a sword, certainly more than a match for most mortal opponents, but against the divine they were as children playing with sticks.

In the arena, Orphus levelled a blinding slash at Emrik, forcing him to disengage, then turned to Merian again. She hid behind her shield, stabbing high and slashing low. The angel waded in to the storm of attacks with dizzying parries. With a flat blade strike to the wrist, he forced Merian to drop her sword, then grabbed her by the shoulder and tossed her towards Emrik like a child would a doll. The twins collided and went down in a heap, metal plates banging and scraping against each other. Orphus stood, relaxed, his sword point resting against the ground.

"Ooooh," Merian groaned loudly. "That's going to bruise." She started to shift herself off her brother.

"Where?" Emrik asked, still lying flat on the ground.

"Everywhere, I think."

"At least it's only a bruise," Emrik said. "I think I broke a rib heroically catching you like that."

Merian laughed. "Any excuse to go have Eleseth heal you, eh?" She finally staggered back to her feet and held out a hand to pull Emrik up.

"Have you seen the way she glows when she touches me? I'm sure she likes me."

Merian finished pulling Emrik to his feet and the twins leaned against each other in silence for a few seconds. Then they charged Orphus as one.

"Fools," Rikkan said with a sigh.

Neither of the twins were armed anymore. They rushed Orphus and the angel calmly spread his wings and with a powerful beat, buffeted them both back to the ground where they sprawled, giggling like children.

Moon clapped loudly. "Quite the dramatic finish. Well done, brother."

Orphus turned, his blue eyes seeming like ice within his helm. "Escaped again, I see, Moon."

"My mind may be a prison, but my body is free." Moon grinned and leaned against Ertide. He was remarkably light. Most angels were all but giants compared to mortals, but Moon was forever trapped in a body of a boy on the cusp of becoming a man.

"Perhaps I should take you back to father?" Orphus said as he dug his sword into the ground and held out his hands, pulling both the twins back to their feet.

Moon shivered. Ertide was sure no one else saw it, but with the angel leaning against him, he felt it.

"Perhaps you should sit on your sword and do a little dance?" Moon gasped and clicked his fingers. "Or better yet. Maybe you should give us a proper show. Fight someone with a bit more punch. Let's see, who could you fight? The mighty Archangel, Sword of Heaven, greatest of all warriors against..." Moon made a show of looking around the sparring grounds before his gaze fell on Rikkan.

"Perfect!" Moon clapped. "The Sword of Heaven versus the Mad Dog of the Crown. That would be quite the show."

"You seek to shame me, brother?" Orphus asked. "I have fought Rikkan many times. I taught him the sword."

"But not the spear," Rikkan said coldly. He leapt over the railing onto the sandy arena and whistled sharply, holding up a hand. One of the nearby soldiers of the First Legion immediately tossed him a spear from the weapon's rack.

Ertide watched as his son pulled off his jacket and tossed it to the floor. He wore no armour, only a plain tunic and trousers, and a pair of leather sandals. He settled down on the balls of his feet, the spear held under one arm, his hand half way up the shaft. Not a soldier's stance, but a duellist's. Orphus plucked his sword from the ground.

Soldiers of the First Legion gathered, quitting their matches and crowding around to watch the show.

"What have you seen, Moon?" Ertide asked.

The Apostle grinned. "A chance."

Rikkan exploded into motion, a series of darting jabs. Orphus gave ground, brushing attacks away, then twisted around a strike and waded forwards. Rikkan leapt away, skidding through the sand to avoid a deadly swipe, then struck back only to be parried aside.

"Are you saying my son can win?" Ertide asked.

Moon scoffed. "No. No one beats the Archangel. Not since the demons of the First Age has anyone seriously challenged him."

In the arena, prince and angel were trading blows so fast Ertide struggled to keep up. It was all a blur to him. Rikkan danced, his spear stabbing. Orphus moved like a bull, his sword a perfect defence against the faster attacks, then struck like a blacksmith hammering an anvil. Rikkan could not block the angel's attacks so skipped away on nimble feet, but he was sweating, panting, slowing down. Orphus pursued relentless, sensing his opponent flagging.

Moon turned his head slowly to look at Ertide, a smile tugging the corner of his mouth. "Why, not in two thousand years has anyone even scored a hit on my brother."

There was a solid gong of metal striking metal, and both combatants froze. Orphus was overextended, his sword mid slice. Rikkan had dropped to one knee, a terrible position, he was all but prone and done for, but his spear tip rested against Orphus' breastplate. A light hit, no more than a tap really, certainly never enough to pierce armour, but it was a hit.

Orphus growled, uncharacteristic frustration echoing from within his helm. He grabbed the spear in one gauntlet and snapped it as easily as a twig. Rikkan stood, calm and still as a frozen pond. Orphus raised his sword and brought it slicing down with an angry cry.

Rikkan didn't move.

Orphus pulled the blow to halt just a breath from Rikkan's neck. Everyone watching knew he could have cleaved the prince in two. But everyone also knew that Rikkan, a mortal, had scored the first hit against the Archangel.

"A chance," Ertide whispered.

Moon was still staring at him. "Every rockslide starts with the subtle shift of a single pebble."

Rikkan stared past the blade hovering at his neck. He gave a slight incline of his head. "The match is yours, angel." He turned and strode from the arena.

The prince had lost the fight, and yet, at that moment, he seemed like the victor.

CHAPTER 8

JERTIS HOVERED OUTSIDE THE DOOR, CLEARLY CONFUSED. Ertide couldn't blame him. The man was his living shadow, following him everywhere, never refused entry to meetings, always a step away to see to his king's needs. But not now. Ertide could only allow those he trusted, those he really trusted into his circle. He closed the door on the servant and turned to the infirmary.

It was a large chamber off to the side of the sparring grounds, filled with beds, tables, all manner of sharp instruments, and most importantly, thick walls. *All the better to muffle the screams of injured patients.*

Moon hopped onto a bed and immediately lay back, his hands behind his head, his wings over his chest like a feathery blanket. Rikkan stood, rigid and ready as he always was. His narrowed eyes darted between Ertide and Moon.

"What is this about, father?" Rikkan asked. "Should I have lost more dutifully to the angel?" He was never very good at keeping the bitter resentment from his voice. It made Ertide's eldest son the perfect conspirator. Everyone already expected him to be sullen, argumentative, and bordering on heresy.

"Are you about to order me to go out there and apologise to Orphus?" His jaw writhed at the thought.

Moon chuckled. "My brother will be apologising to you soon enough," the angel said. "Next time he won't take it so easy on you."

Rikkan turned a dangerous stare on Moon that the angel didn't even notice. "Take it easy on me? I just showed everyone that angels are not infallible. You can be beaten."

Moon sat up and shifted his wings so they draped either side of the bed. "Now which of us is the fool?"

"Careful, angel."

Moon chuckled. "If Orphus had wanted to, he would have waded through your impotency and crushed your skull regardless of how thick it might be. You landed a hit?" He clapped his hands slowly. "Well done, you. Truly an accomplishment that should be sung for the ages. Hark! Here comes Rikkan, the mighty Shield of Empire whose crowning achievement was forcing an angel to pause and polish his armor. No no, don't mock him, he's very proud. Much like a dog that shits on the carpet then struts about like its done an art."

"I should cut your head off, angel."

"If only you could. But there in lies the problem, my dear Fool of Empire. For all your skill and all your strength, even if you had found the most perfect chink in Orphus' armour, that spear of yours could never even pierce his skin. Not while his immortality shield is intact."

"What?"

Ertide pulled up a chair. It was hard and wobbly, certainly not meant for any prolonged sitting, but it would do. "What sort of infirmary doesn't have wine? I could do with something to wash down the heresy."

Rikkan turned to him, eyes narrowed. "What is this about, father?"

Ertide glanced at Moon. The angel shrugged back. "Tell him, Moon."

"How much?"

"Start at the beginning."

"Your father is dying."

Rikkan spun, glaring at Ertide. "What? How? Were you injured?"

Ertide sighed. "The beginning, Moon."

"Oh, right. God can't hear you."

Rikkan waved an angry hand towards Moon and sat down opposite

Ertide. "Father, you're dying?" He shook his head. "You're not allowed to die. Stop it."

Ertide chuckled. It turned to a raspy cough, icy hands clawing into his chest. He coughed bright red into his handkerchief. Rikkan stared at it with wide, wild eyes. It took Ertide a minute to get his breathing back under control, to stop feeling like there were hands reaching up from the darkness and smothering him.

"Son, listen to me. To us," Ertide said. "God cannot hear us."

Rikkan sent a pointed glance at Moon, then back to Ertide, a meaningful shake of his head.

"It's true," Moon said happily, still sitting on the bed, his legs crossed beneath him. "He can watch through the eyes of his children, but not all at once. He is not omnipresent, though he very much wants you to believe he is. "

"This is a trap, father," Rikkan said. "The angels have been wanting rid of you for a long time now. This is just an excuse, to get you to admit to heresy. He..." Rikkan threw out a hand and pointed at Moon. "Cannot be trusted."

Time to take control. Be the general, not the doddering old king.

"Enough!" Ertide hissed. "Moon can be trusted. I trust him with my life."

"Ahhh, that's sweet."

Ertide turned an angry stare on his friend. "It is important to understand, son, what I have said out loud, and to Moon, even here, is already enough to be considered heresy. If God can hear me, the angels would be breaking down that door and gagging me before dragging me off to my execution. And yet, they do not. God's omnipresence is a lie he has purposefully spread."

"Why?"

Moon laughed. "Think about it, Prince Grumpy. What better way to completely subdue an entire people than to convince them you see all, know all. Speak out and God will know and off with his head."

Rikkan shook his head. "What does this have to do with your dying, father?"

Ertide softened into a sad smile. "Age catches up with me, son. A silent predator I cannot escape. Not on my own." He glanced over at the angel.

Moon slipped from the bed and slinked closer on silent feet. He pulled up a final chair and sat facing Ertide and Rikkan.

"I can save him," the angel said quietly. "But before I go any further, you both need to understand something. The dangers."

All trace of Moon's usual joviality fled. The young man sitting before them was sombre. "The God is not merciful, and he guards his secrets with a ruthless jealousy. If I tell this secret, and if he finds out, he will destroy you. And he will destroy anyone he even suspects may also know."

"What does that mean?" Rikkan asked.

"It means, I will be leveraging my entire family against my own life," Ertide said slowly. "If one of us knows this secret, he will assume we all do."

"He must," Moon agreed.

Rikkan shook his head. "The Hostain family has served the God for over two thousand years. Our ancestors built this damned empire for him."

"And yet," Moon said, spreading his hands. "He will not hesitate to stamp you out. He would raze this entire city to the ground, eradicate every man, woman, child, cat, dog, flea, everything to keep this secret."

Rikkan narrowed his eyes, and looked to Ertide. He respected his son for that. A weaker man would have demanded to know. But Rikkan held true to his own convictions. He would follow his father's lead wherever that took him. It made him an excellent son, but it would also make him a terrible king.

Ertide nodded to Moon.

"Angel blood," Moon said quietly. "It can save your life, extend it, give you back the strength age has stolen from you. Angel blood can grant a human immortality."

Ertide sat back in his chair, considering. *Father wrote there is a strength in blood. Did he know?*

"Well, why do we hesitate?" Rikkan asked. He pulled a knife from his belt, flicked it around until he was holding the blade and held it out to Moon. "Open a vein and save him."

Moon snatched the knife and tossed it up, catching it with two fingers around the naked blade. "Ahh, my good Prince Stabs-Alot, if only it was so simple. If any angel gives you their blood willingly, God will know, and his smiting will be ruinous. It must be taken, not given."

"Fine," Rikkan snarled. "Father, I'll hold this fool down, you leech him."

"So simple, your mind. No blade you can forge will pierce my skin," Moon said. "We angels are made of sturdy stuff."

Ertide thought about it. He'd trained for many years with angels, he fought beside them in countless battles. Had he ever seen an angel bleed? Yes. He remembered clearly the Battle of the Vale. He stood side by side with the Rider as the barbarian hordes had charged down from the rocky passes. They had killed so many. Bodies piled high, bloated and floating in the flood pass. The Rider had taken an axe to the skull. He shrugged it off, ran his lightning wreathed sword through the wielder, but there had been blood dripping down his perfect face. What had been different? What had weakened the Rider so much then that a simple axe could pierce his skin?

Rikkan growled in frustration. "If you cannot give us blood, and we cannot take it, then what is the point of this conversation?"

"There must be a way around this immortality shield," Ertide said, his mind still working.

"Or a way to break it," Moon said. "I need time. Things need to be put in place, people moved across the board."

"How long does my father have?"

Moon's face crumpled. "A year at most." He gave Ertide a look of such compassion. "It is going to get worse, much worse, before we can make it better. I am sorry."

Ertide shook his head. "Suffering is a whetstone to hone a man's will."

Moon reached out and squeezed Ertide's hand. His small act of comfort was shield against the pain Ertide knew was to come.

"Make no moves until I return," Moon said. "But gather allies to you. Only those whose trust is beyond doubt. There can be no question to their loyalty. It must be to you, not to God."

"Family first," Ertide said. "The twins?"

"No!" Moon said too quickly. "Not them."

Rikkan glared at the angel. "Why not? What is wrong with my children?"

"Just... not the twins. Not Emrik. You have to trust me on this."

Rikkan's jaw writhed, but he looked to Ertide for his course.

"Gather your allies," Moon said again. "You will need soldiers you can trust, command. Those would lay down their lives for you. Those who have already begun to doubt the angels' invulnerability. And Ertide, my old friend, you must give my brothers and sisters no cause for suspicion. Play the doddering king a while longer. Build Mathanial's ships, give him whatever he wants."

Ertide hissed. "He'll beggar the bloody empire."

"My brother is quick to anger, and quick to forget, but if you continue to push him, he will remove you. And God will do nothing. If that happens, all is lost." His eyes went distant, not dark like he was lost in his visions, but far away. "You must be king, old friend. You must remain king."

CHAPTER 9

Weeks passed and Ertide heard nothing from Moon. The Apostle had flown away in the night, promising he would return shortly. But Ertide was not so certain. His friend disappeared for months or even years at a time, not even remembering where he had been, and with no notion of how long he had been gone. It was the curse of his seer's sight, unstuck through time.

Rikkan moved slowly, taking close stock of all his soldiers from the First Legion, those who protected city and palace. A lot of guardsmen found their duties changed, the positions they had held for so long, suddenly awarded to others. It was more subtle than Ertide had realised his son was capable of. Slowly, but surely, people they could trust unfailingly were moved into the palace.

Despite the treason, the heresy taking root within his empire, at his own command, Ertide found himself with little to do. He had his duties as king, making appearances to keep the nobility happy, sitting judge on crimes, moving the empire's resources about to pay for the various projects placed in front of him. It was all so tedious now. He longed to move, to take action, to be the general again, not the bureaucrat. But he could not. His body failed him.

Day after day, the icy claws in his chest grew sharper, colder, more insistent. He burned a dozen handkerchiefs a day to keep the evidence of his infirmity a secret. Even light exercise tired him and he could not catch his breath. Ylnaea noticed. How could she not? She came to his bed chambers nightly, as was God's will. She saw the blood he coughed up, the tenderness in his movements. He tried to pass it off as a cold, a brief illness and nothing more, but he could see in her guarded gaze she was not convinced. Ertide knew it would not be long before she revealed his secret to the angels. He was not sure what they would do when they found out.

He took to spending lengthy periods in the King's Shrine. It was a place of solitude, where he could hide from others, human and angel, and from his responsibilities. No one dared set foot in the shrine, and if the king spent longer than he used to inside, well that just showed his newly recuperated piousness.

The city bells rang out to call an end to the morning prayers. The noise was like nails being hammered into Ertide's head, but he tried his best to ignore them. He had the window thrown open despite the pouring rain outside, just in case Moon chose to return. Rain splashed in through the window, but it didn't reach him. Ertide had cleared away much of the dust, and had replaced the burnt out candles. He'd also dragged a proper table and chair into the shrine so he was more comfortable in his studies.

He had his father's old copy of the Rite of the Divine, a few sheets of paper, and an ink pot and pen. The notes he made paled in comparison to those his father had scrawled on the holy text. Not a page in the book had escaped Terin Hostain's scrutiny, and much of it was calling into question events, debating certain practices, citations for further reading and comparisons of versions of the truth.

The book was open on the ninety-second page, an account of the time directly proceeding the war against the demons, just three decades before the Second Age was rung in by the angel Eleseth. The passage read:

The Saint returned to her people victorious. The enemies of God vanquished, human and angelkind united to form a new alliance against the lingering darkness.

Terin had put a hastily scrawled note next to it:

What lingering darkness? Enemies of God NOT vanquished? And then underneath that another note added later: *Bone Reaver. See page 212.*

Further down the same page: *On the site of their new home, of the great jewel that was soon to be the Holy City of Celesgarde, the Saint gave birth to her first child. From that glorious deliverance sprang the staunchest allies of heaven, the protectors of mankind.*

There was a flurry of notes around that paragraph: *First child? No mention of second. Was there another?* And: *Who was the father? No mention. Where else does the Hostain line begin?* And: *Divergence? See page 426 of Rook's Compendium. Where was Helena Hostain born?*

Ertide made a note of Rook's Compendium to seek it out later. It seemed his father's notes had often been to point out inconsistencies, sometimes within the book, and other times written down in different books. Ertide was no scholar, but he was starting to see what his father had wanted to show him. Something was wrong about the history of the Sant Dien Empire. It didn't add up.

He flicked through the book to page two-hundred-and-twelve, and started reading until he came to his father's first note. The text read:

God could no longer abide the devilry of Tarkum Chaim. His people were threatened, their souls ripped from their bodies, forced to serve for eternity. It was long said that when the bone chariot rattled across the sky, even the insects crawled in fear. The God summoned his greatest angels, his most loyal Knights Exemplar, and marched upon the Lonesome Isle.

The notes here were written in a more crabbed style. Ertide could see his father wasting away as he wrote them, his hands losing their dexterity.

Tarkum Chaim? Bone chariot? The Bone Reaver? What lies in the Lonesome Isle? Ancient darkness?

Ertide pinched the bridge of his nose and screwed his eyes shut. The Lonesome Isle lay to the northwest, beyond the land and beyond the ice. It was forbidden by God, no one to set foot there. Even the Ice Walkers, who sailed farther out than anyone in the Sant Dien Empire, never went close to the Lonesome Isle.

There was a knock at the door. Ertide gave them permission to enter and then the knock repeated. He suddenly remembered he was in the King's Shrine and no one was allowed entry. He tucked the book away, trapping his newly scrawled notes inside, between the pages, then pushed the book under the pew where a shadowy alcove would hide it. When he finally ambled over to the door, he found Arandon waiting there looking a little dishevelled.

His grandson leaned to the side a little, staring past Ertide into the shrine. "Heaven's Light, Grandfather."

Ertide grunted noncommittally. He might have to hide his heresy for now, but had decided he would take whatever little acts of rebellion he could.

"Your carriage is here."

"Excellent," Ertide pushed past his grandson and pulled the door shut behind him, locking it and pocketing the key. Jertis watched, yet said nothing. Until a few weeks ago, Ertide had let his servant carry the key. Now he didn't trust anyone else to hold on to it. The contents were too dangerous.

Arandon paced easily alongside Ertide, proof that he was slowing down. The icy claws in his chest made him run out of breath quickly and the only way to hide it was to slow his pace.

"Demon to Exemplar three," Ertide said as they walked. They had recently started a new game of *Clash* after Arandon had won their previous by dominion. There were two ways to win a game; dominion involved capturing six of the seven shrines scattered across the board. Domination was a far more straight forward method. If your opponent didn't have enough pieces to hold six shrines, they couldn't win, so you did by default.

"A bold opening gambit, Grandfather," Arandon said. "But one that leaves..."

Ertide held up a hand for silence. "Do you know what I've always found odd about Clash? How unequal it is. The pieces, you see, the rules they move by. The light side seems to have such an advantage. The angel can move across almost the entire board and can strike at multiple pieces at once. Undoubtedly the most powerful piece in the game. But on the dark side, the pieces use very different rules and therefore different strategies. The wulfkin can move together, travelling as a pack. And yet on both sides, there are soldiers. The weakest pieces on the board and the most numerous, serving both the light and dark."

Arandon chuckled. "Did your loss affect you so severely, Grandfather, that you felt the need to brush up on the basics? I am allowed to win occasionally."

"Perhaps it's just my age, Arandon. The mind begins to wander."

The palace was alive with activity, beyond the usual hustle and bustle, preparations were underway for Caran's birthday. Ertide's third son was always such a flamboyant fool, demanding a grand celebration each year. There would be food and wine and music and dancing. The whole family was invited, though most were far too busy elsewhere in the empire. Nobility would flock to the palace and the entire spectacle would cost enough to beggar a small town. But it was necessary. Appearances had to be maintained.

"Where are we going, Grandfather?" Arandon asked. He flicked through the notes on his board. "You have meetings with the Ice Isles representative today and…"

"Cancel it," Ertide said. "I haven't the time."

Arandon cleared his throat. "You've cancelled the meeting six times already."

"They're playing us, Grandson," Ertide said. "These Ice Walkers have been in my city for three weeks now living off the crown's generosity. Each time we meet they ask the impossible, tariffs that would make a whore blanch. There is no give in them, only take."

"We do need their leviathan oil, Grandfather," Arandon said. "There really is no substitute. Something about the potency, I hear."

"Yes, we do." Ertide stopped at the bottom of the staircase as much to catch his breath as to make his point. He reached over and flipped Arandon's notes down. The man spent too long staring at figures and not nearly enough time looking at people. He knew how to strategise, to play games like Clash, but he had never spent time with soldiers. Soldiers liked to gamble, and the game these Ice Walkers were playing was one of bluffs and bullying.

"We need them, but not as much as they need us. Our trade. Who else but us will the Ice Walkers trade their oil to? The barbarians? That's a long way to sail with highly flammable oil in the hold, and the only port is the Watch, which belongs to us. They'd have to pay us to sell their oil to Aelegar. This is all a bluff. They'll hold out for as long as possible, setting the same impossible demands again and again, hoping we'll give in. We won't. Eventually they compromise."

Arandon frowned. "Don't you always say compromise is just another form of capitulation?"

"Exactly," Ertide clapped his grandson on the shoulder. "Now come on, we are going to Arkenhold."

CHAPTER 10

Arkenhold was the largest and most prestigious of the four universities in Celesgarde. People from all over the Sant Dien Empire applied to study within its labyrinthine halls, but each year only a select number were admitted. Arkenhold led the way in fields of study like metallurgy, archaeology, geology, alchemy, and more recently they were making large strides in unlocking the power of flight for humanity.

Previously, the domain of the sky had been jealously guarded by the angels. Their wings made them masters of the air, and they had a strange command of the pegasi, too, so that the winged horses would not allow a human rider without express permission. But the Age of Exploration demanded new methods of exploring the world, and the bright minds at Arkenhold had come up with the Skydrifter.

The Skydrifter was still very much in its early stages of development, but controlled test flights were happening every few weeks now. None of those tests had proven particularly successful yet, though the professors of Airology at Arkenhold were confident they were making progress.

Ertide locked his knees to stop the trembling weakness in his legs from becoming apparent, and watched the huge balloon slowly inflate as the assistants pumped some sort of substance into it. At sufficient volume, the balloon rose into the air, dragging a small basket with it. A young woman wearing goggles stood in the basket, waving a hand in the air as the balloon dragged it upwards. The whole thing was tethered to the ground to stop it from floating away. The professor declared the test a resounding success, no doubt to demand more funds in the near future.

At first, the Rider had come to the test flights to observe. It was his dream, after all. A fleet of balloons, each carrying hundreds of humans and supplies aplenty, flying alongside the winged angels and pegasi. Mathanial's interest had swiftly waned when he realised it would take time to reach such a level of success.

As Ertide watched, a young man shimmied up the tether and climbed into the basket. The balloon began to sink back to the ground, too heavily weighted. Far from being able to carry hundreds of people, it could barely lift one.

The wizened professor made some excuses, rattling off numbers and equations, and claiming increasing the volume of the balloon would have exponential results. Ertide asked if he had solved the problem of directing the flight. As of now, the Skydrifters were reliant on the whims of the wind, blown wherever it would go. The professor mumbled out a few terms Ertide did not understand as a way of saying *no*.

The test might be a success, but the project was still a failure. Ertide decided to cut funding and hoped the Rider would either not notice or not care. His boats were being built, and that would have to be enough.

He strode through the university grounds with Arandon and a host of servants in tow. Hundreds of students and professors milled about the halls, attending classes or having vain philosophical debates. It made Ertide smile. He'd attended Arkenhold himself for two years, studying military history and theory. He'd had no use for the more academic subjects, but those with more applicable reasoning had been useful. As a youth, he'd studied at the feet of humans and angels both, and later he had put everything he'd learned into practice on the battlefield.

Yet one thing had always bothered him. Every battle he had won, every war fought, and every rebellion crushed, had all been thanks to the angels. Without their strength and invulnerability, his forces might have been smashed. Bereft of their mobility and devastating powers, most of his tactics would have failed. The empire was so large, so sprawling, that they couldn't maintain and protect it without help from the angels.

Even something so simple as communication. It would take days to send a message to Vael on the coast, even with the messenger regularly swapping horses and riding through the night. It would take many weeks to send a message all the way to Bresh in the Ashlands, especially as no messenger but an angel could climb over the Cracked Mountains. Even angels didn't dare try to cross the Fangs on foot. And so they had the divine messenger service, angels who ferried reports back and forth across the empire. But how did Ertide know the reports they delivered were the same as those he sent? It would be easy for them to alter the orders within.

It bothered Ertide how entirely reliant they were on angels for so many aspects of life and of ruling the empire. But he saw no way to take the power they had ceded back without crippling the empire.

The grand oak doors to the Arkenhold library stood open. It had been that way for as long as he could remember. The library was open to all students and professors, their access unrestricted. *Almost unrestricted. There were always books even I was encouraged away from.*

His entrance to the library caused quite a stir. Students looked up from their studies, whispers echoed down the stacks, and within moments Oronesus glided down on her hawk wings from the balcony above. Of course, Ertide had expected his visit would not go unnoticed.

"Heaven's Light, Ertide." The Bookkeeper's smile was radiant. "It has been a long time since you last graced the stacks.

Ertide plastered on the doddering smile he'd come to wear so well. "I seem to have caused a bit of a stir. I'm sorry, Oronesus."

"It's certainly not every day the king comes to Arkenhold. I imagine many of our students have never even seen you before."

Ertide grunted. *Such pageantry. As if I am a specimen to be put on display. Here we have the very picture of an impotent king. See how we long ago clipped his metaphorical wings.*

"Are you here for a book?" Oronesus asked, a frown creasing her too beautiful face. "I keep the palace library well stocked."

Yes, well stocked with approved volumes. Only the most pious of literature for the king.

Ertide strode past the angel, his retinue trailing behind, towards the stacks. Arkenhold library was the largest in the west. "Yes, I thought I'd do some research like I used to." He scratched at his beard and turned a smile on Oronesus.

The Bookkeeper's face lit up with delight. "Wonderful. Do you have a subject in mind? I am always happy to direct seekers to the knowledge they desire."

"Hmmm." He had thought about this, knowing Oronesus would question and monitor him. He needed a subject that was bland enough it wouldn't raise suspicion. "I was thinking of the Knights Exemplar. I haven't forgotten that the Grand Samir courtyard still needs that renovation, and it dawned on me while in prayer just yesterday that to decide on the particular design from the ideas the guild sent me, I should really know a bit more about this Samir fellow. Who was he? Why did he follow the Saint?"

"Ahh, a fascinating topic." Oronesus extended her stride a little to get ahead of them, then waved towards a flight of stairs leading to the first balcony. "This way to one of our more secluded alcoves. I have just the tome you're looking for, Ertide. Two hundred years ago, Karsol Weathers collected every scrap of information he could about the Exemplars and wrote an excellent treatise on it, detailing what is known and what is known to be false. I'm told he interviewed Orphus and a number of other angels from the First Age to get the best possible view of the six Exemplars. I've read the treatise myself and it is quite fascinating."

Yes, no doubt. And I'm sure every word in the book was painstakingly vetted.

"That sounds just what I'm looking for."

Oronesus led him to an alcove and he sat and waited while food and wine was brought to him. Neither were typically allowed in the library, but there were some perks to being king, he supposed. Eventually Oronesus returned with the promised tome and set about directing Ertide to the relevant sections. Ertide skimmed through them, but they were predictably vague about much of the Exemplar's life, and even more so about his death. There was no mention of a war against Tarkum Chaim. Oronesus hovered, not leaving his side, making specific note every time he turned a page. It was maddening to be so watched. He needed to get her to leave.

Ertide closed his eyes and let his hands go limp, slouching in his chair. He faked a soft snore and ignored the people fretting around him. *There has to be some benefit to getting old.*

Oronesus paced, her footfalls heavier than anyone else. Eventually she whispered a few words to Arandon, then hurried away. Ertide let the slightest smile creep onto his lips.

"Just what are you up to, Grandfather?" Arandon said. "You can stop pretending to be asleep now, she's gone."

Ertide cracked open an eye. In the flickering lantern light, Arandon sat across from him, his face stern. Jertis was nearby somewhere, just waiting to be summoned, but the rest of the servants had gone. Ertide sat up straight, hating how his back ached from slumping, and pushed the useless book away. He wasn't going to find what he was looking for in those overly approved pages.

"Have you ever heard of Tarkum Chaim?" Ertide asked.

Arandon shook his head. "Is it a person? A place? A mushroom? Give me a hint, Grandfather."

"A demon, maybe?" Ertide said. "Some great enemy of the God. What about the Bone Reaver?"

Arandon frowned at that. "The Reaver piece in Clash is sometimes depicted as a man with the skull of a hound over his head. What is this about?"

"What indeed?" Ertide said, smiling. "Find me a book, Arandon. Rook's Compendium."

"Why, Grandfather?"

Ertide stood so sharply, white spots danced in his eyes and he felt dizzy. "Because I just ordered you to."

Arandon sighed, held his gaze for a few moments, then stood and stalked off in search of the book. Jertis slunk out of the dark, looking a little worried.

"Anything I can get you, my king?"

Ertide grumbled. "Better wine? This crap tastes like it was brewed in a privy."

Jertis smiled and bowed, then scurried off.

Ertide waited for a few moments, until he was sure Jertis and all the rest of his minders were gone, then hurried off into the stacks. He had another book to find, one he was certain the angels didn't want him to read.

CHAPTER 11

The archive was on the top level of the Arkenhold University library. Essentially it was a vault where the oldest, and often most delicate, texts were kept. No students or professors were allowed in there without express permission from an angel. And as the library was Oronesus' domain, that meant she controlled who did and did not get to view those oldest books. But Ertide was king of the Sant Dien Empire, not a student or a professor. He needed no permission to go anywhere in his own lands.

Ertide was out of breath and trembling by the time he reached the top of the stairs. He had to clutch to the bannister to stop from collapsing. The icy claws in his chest were creeping closer to his heart, and his breath rasped in and out of his chest like bellows with a ripped lung. Onwards, he struggled, coughing into a handkerchief as he went. At least there was no blood this time.

The archive was at the end of a dingily lit corridor just past the last bookshelf. Most of the books on this floor were undocumented texts waiting to be assigned relevance by Oronesus.

Waiting to be vetted to ensure the contents are suitable for those of us living in ignorance.

"If you wanted a book from up here, Grandfather, you should have just sent me," Arandon said from ahead. Ertide peered into the gloom and it took a few seconds for his eyes to adjust. His grandson was sitting calmly on a chair at the end of the bookshelves. He did not have a copy of Rook's Compendium with him.

Ertide chuckled. "You guessed I'd be coming up here?"

"You've never been one to send others to do what you yourself are capable of, Grandfather. And..." He sighed and stood, smoothing down his robe. "Despite what my father thinks, I'm no fool. You're hunting something. Knowledge. I don't for one moment believe it's as simple as wanting to know about Knight Exemplar Samir to build his bloody courtyard anew."

Ertide stopped before his grandson and peered at the man's face. Soft features, so unlike his father. His skin, too, was a shade lighter than any of the Hostains. Arandon never fit in. Not with his father, not with his brothers or sisters. The twins barely even acknowledged his existence. But he had a keen mind, and the one place he had always fit was by Ertide's side. By his king's side.

But can I trust him? Smart as an owl, maybe, but also never misses a prayer. He bows to the angels far deeper than he does to me. And besides, Moon said not to trust any of Rikkan's children.

Ertide smiled benignly. "You're never too old to stop learning, Arandon." He started past his grandson, into the dingy corridor. Two soldiers in black and gold waited at the far end before an unassuming door.

"I've been thinking on my next move," Ertide said as he walked. "Second soldier to Shrine Five."

"A weak position and clearly a distraction. What aren't you telling me, Grandfather?"

Ertide stopped and turned sharply. "A lot of things. I am the king of the Sant Dien Empire, Arandon, not you. I am not required to explain myself to you or anyone." The icy hands clawed further up his chest, and he felt a bony finger poke a single spot of frost into his heart.

Arandon bowed his head in supplication. "I'm sorry, Grandfather. I didn't mean to suggest..." He sank to one knee. "I am sorry, my king."

Ertide stared down at his grandson in disgust. He'd never made any of his family bow like that. He hated himself for doing it now.

Hold to your family above all else for there is power in blood. His own father's words in that final note he had left. Family should always support each other, respect each other. And here he was demeaning his own grandchild.

"Get up, Arandon," Ertide said, holding out a hand. Arandon needed no help, but he took Ertide's hand all the same and beamed an uncharacteristic smile.

The soldiers guarding the door glanced at each other when their king approached, then bowed their heads in unison. It did not escape Ertide's notice that neither moved from in front of the door.

"This is the archive, sire," one of the soldiers, a woman with pale skin and mousy hair, said.

"I'm well aware. Get out of the way."

Again that shared glance.

"Oronesus has long-standing orders that no one but her may—"

"Oronesus is king now?" Arandon said sharply.

"I... Uh..." The soldier stammered and kept her head bowed.

Arandon took a step past Ertide and stood over the soldier. "Your orders come from the king, not from an angel. You serve the crown, not heaven. Stand aside."

A moment's hesitation.

They're deciding whether to disobey me. Either through respect or fear, they serve heaven as surely as they do me. This is how far my authority has fallen.

He remembered his old military doctrine studies. Control of the military *is* control of the state. All systems of governance were held up by three pillars. The crown's pillars were the military, communication, and history.

The angels already had control of communication. They had for generations now. The empire was entirely reliant upon them to reach its outer holdings.

Control of the military is slipping. When did it start? Surely before me. My father was a weak commander, a scholar at heart. He bent to every demand heaven placed upon him.

Ertide also remembered sitting at his father's bedside as the old man wasted away. He was delirious, ranting, often in a language Ertide didn't know. But one thing he had said stood out to Ertide.

I tried. I tried. You cannot separate crown and divine.

Yet, Terin Hostain had never tried to stand up to heaven. He had given in to their every demand. Never once saying *no*. Ertide remembered because he had always thought his father was weak for it. He had always tried to be different, to resist divine decrees wherever he could because his father had not.

I have done this. I kept trying to separate crown and heaven without even realising I was doing it, and I have made us all weak because of it.

"Grandfather?" Arandon said.

Ertide blinked, realising he'd been lost in his own thoughts like a dog chasing its own tail. The soldiers were standing aside. Whatever Arandon had said to them had made them stand down. He straightened his back and opened the door to the vault.

The archive was three large rooms without decoration or windows. Arandon had to fetch a lantern for them to see anything. The first room was lined with tables at every wall. The second was stacked with bookshelves. And the third room was filled with wooden crates. All were empty, bare. No books on the shelves. The crates filled with nothing but a thin trail of dust. The tables held some scrapes and dents, but not a single book or scroll in sight. The archive was empty.

Ertide stood staring at the bare bookshelves in the flickering light of Arandon's lantern. He drew in a deep breath of stale air and felt another icy claw touch his heart.

"Is it possible Oronesus finished cataloguing them all?" Arandon asked.

Ertide shook his head slowly. The archive was meant to house books too delicate to be kept in the general areas of the library. "Anything that was kept here has either been moved or destroyed."

"What? Why would they destroy books?"

Ertide turned a tired stare on his grandson. "History is mutable, written not by the hand of relevance, but instead by those with ink to spare."

"Ink..." Arandon mused.

What are they hiding? What part of our history, of us, have they altered to fit their needs?

A soft clearing of the throat sounded from the first room. Ertide spun about too quickly, his vision swimming. Oronesus stood in the room with the tables, her eyes narrowed, wings twitching.

The icy hands were back, clutching at Ertide's heart. He couldn't breathe. Couldn't breathe. He pulled at his chest with his right hand. His entire left side felt like it was on fire.

"If there were more specific rare texts you wanted, you really should have told me," Oronesus said, her voice unyielding as stone.

Arandon stepped forward. "Where have all the books gone? Why is the vault empty?"

Oronesus gave an incredulous smile and shook her head. "The vault has been empty for years. The sturdier texts were moved into the library general, while the more delicate works were long ago transferred to Heaven's Library where they can be cared for and preserved. This was..." She frowned. "Ertide?"

"Grandfather?"

I can't breathe. I can't breathe!

Ertide saw the floor rushing up to meet him, and then nothing.

CHAPTER 12

Ertide lay in bed and waited. Hazy morning light crept around the burgundy curtains, giving his bedroom a warm glow. He stared at the grand tapestry of the Saint and her Knights Exemplars and their angelic allies, charging into battle against the demon hordes. The greatest battle for humanity, to free them from the thralldom of demon bondage. The demons seemed unassailable, their horde endless, their forms savage, mutilated twists on humans and beasts. But the angels and the Exemplars had light on their side; shining armour, divine weapons forged in Heaven's armoury, each with its own power. The Saint herself carried a giant hammer, molten veins running through the metal.

Ertide had fought many battles in his youth, but he knew none of them would be remembered with anything like as much reverence or significance. Every battle he had ever fought had been with angels by his side, and other humans arrayed against him. The demons were all dead.

A part of him wished the demons were still around, that his battles had been against them instead. *At least then I'd have been sure I was fighting on the right side.*

He cleared his throat, tasted blood on his lips. Just yesterday, Eleseth had come to visit him and had laid her healing hands on his chest. She was radiant beyond light itself and glowed with the warmth of a forge fire. She'd smiled at him so kindly as she cupped his cheek and told him she was sorry. He'd known it was over then. Not even Eleseth could heal him. He really was dying.

"Age," the Herald of the Second Age had said. "There is no wound or illness eating away at you, Ertide, my old friend. There comes a time when mortal flesh and blood fail. When the body no longer knows how to repair itself. Your body is too taxed, your heart is giving out. I am sorry. All you can do now is rest, and enjoy what time you have left. Spend it with your family, your children, those you love most. And when the time comes." She smiled so sadly. "Soon. My father will welcome you into heaven."

He had almost asked her then whether Moon had spoken true. Whether angel blood could save him. But Moon's warning was too dire. If the Apostle was correct and angel blood could grant immortality, God would slaughter anyone who might know. And he would start with the Hostain dynasty. So instead, Ertide had thanked Eleseth for all she had done and sank back into his bed to await death.

Where are you Moon? Come back to me.

"Jertis," Ertide called out. Not loudly. He couldn't manage loud anymore.

The door creaked open and Jertis peered through the gap. As soon as he saw Ertide was awake, he bustled into the room like a storm in summer, upsetting the stillness. The man kept up a steady barrage of conversation as he moved about.

"How are you feeling?

"You're looking better today, sire. More colour in your cheeks.

"The bards arrived this morning and there's already been a fight including a broken lute. I thought a fight between bards would be all eloquent retorts and thumbing noses. Oh, how wrong I was. One man threw down his floppy hat, then beat the other to the floor, broke his lute over his head, then kicked until the poor fellow was spitting teeth."

It maddened Ertide. Jertis had never been one for inane chatter, but now Ertide was broken he filled the air around him with noise. At the same time, Ertide was glad for it. The noise reminded him he was still alive. On his way out, but not gone yet. Not quite yet.

Jertis helped him sit, then fussed about with a damp cloth, wiping down his sweaty skin. Then he laid out a suit of royal blue with orange threads. It had the effect of almost making Ertide look healthy again. *Almost.*

The truth was it was embarrassing that he needed such help washing and dressing, even sitting up in bed. But there was little else to be done. His left arm no longer worked, he could barely even feel it. His legs wobbled constantly and he had to lean on a cane to even shuffle about. He had once been mighty, the feared Crimson Prince. Now he was a decaying shell, quickly crumbling to dust.

With Jertis on one side, and his cane propping him up on the other, Ertide shuffled out of his bedroom and into his sitting room. It exhausted him and he slumped down onto his sofa with a weary sigh. The usual banquet of a breakfast was brought in and he picked at a few pieces of fruit, but he had no appetite. Everything tasted too sweet or too greasy or dry.

"What happens to the food, Jertis?" Ertide asked as he leaned back and glanced at the mound of untouched breakfast.

"Sire?"

"All the food I don't eat every day. Where does it go? What happens to it?"

"I don't know for certain, sire."

"Hmm. Make sure it's eaten, Jertis. If by nobody in the palace, have it taken into the city to feed the poor. I'd hate to know so much is going to waste." Ertide drew in a deep breath, felt the icy claw like a cage around his heart. "What's on the cards today, Jertis?"

"Sire. Nothing."

Ertide snorted.

"Prince Caran has been dealing with much of the day-to-day decision making for the realm while you were convalescing, but his celebration is tonight and so all meetings have been postponed. There will be the celebration this evening, of course. I will be by your side should you wish to attend."

"The celebration, of course." Many of his family would be there. Angels, too, and the nobility. Caran's birthday was always such an event.

"Where is Arandon?" Ertide asked suddenly. It seemed strange that his grandson wouldn't be involved in the day-to-day decisions of the crown.

"Prince Arandon set off for the Ice Isles, Sire. He's travelling with the ambassador to further discussions of the leviathan oil trade."

Ertide frowned at that. There were no discussions to be had, further or otherwise. He'd already told Arandon they were to hold out until the Ice Walkers caved. And to travel all the way north to the ice to no end. Something smelled wrong about it.

"Let's just hope he doesn't give away half the empire in tariffs, hmm?"

"Yes, sire."

CHAPTER 13

THE NIGHT OF CARAN'S BIRTHDAY CELEBRATION ARRIVED, and the palace lit up with noise and activity. Decorative banners hung from every balcony and sill. The old carpets were bundled away and replaced with new, vibrantly colourful rugs. Statues of Hostains long dead and angels who still lived were rolled out of some storage room or other and lined the halls. Bards set up at all the entrances to welcome guests with a cacophony of intermingling noise.

It all gave Ertide a headache.

The city was in a state of celebration, too. The people were taking their cue from their rulers. There was dancing and singing and merry-making in the streets. Every church was handing out free wine, and the taverns were overflowing. The entire city of Celesgarde was a bustle.

"How can we afford it all, I wonder?" Ertide mused as Jertis fussed about his tunic and jacket, getting them to sit just right.

"Does it matter, Sire?" the man asked. "Everyone seems very happy."

"Well of course it matters, Arandon..." Ertide paused and shook his head. Arandon was gone, away with the Ice Walkers, and had been for weeks now. Ever since his feinting, his mind had been getting more and more cloudy. He didn't like it. He felt drunk even without a drink.

Jertis said nothing about the slip. The man stopped fussing and opened the box on the table, pulling out the heavy black iron crown.

"Of course it matters," Ertide repeated. "Can't have them beggaring the empire for the sake of a party." He'd been frozen out of all matters since his feinting. The empire rolled on without him; his duties, his decisions, his power all scooped up by others. He truly was a king in name only these days.

Jertis stepped up behind Ertide and slowly lowered the crown atop his head. "Perfect," the servant said.

Ertide only grumbled in reply. He'd always hated wearing the crown. It seemed such an ostentatious thing. He didn't need a circlet to prove he was king. People should just know.

Jertis had to help him from his rooms and down the stairs. Even with his cane, Ertide was unstable these days. But his servant was always just a step away, hovering in case he was needed. Ertide was grateful for that, even as he lamented the need.

The celebration was in full swing in the palace. Guests roamed about, drinking and talking and probably scheming. Many were the nobility and merchants from Celesgarde, those who were wealthy enough to secure their invitations. Some were from out of town. Ertide recognised the Breen's from Gurrand, their brood swarming about their feet. Eight children over seven years, and Tilda Breen was already fat with number nine. He greeted them with a smile and laughed as the horde of little Breen's danced about him for a few seconds until their parents corralled them. Ertide also recognised Fansis Keel, the shipwright from Vael. He was alone and chatting to a number of Celesgarde merchants, and one towering First Age angel encased in shining silver armour. Keel had gotten rich off the crown these past few years, owning the largest ship construction company in the empire. The oily man spotted Ertide and raised a glass of wine, a smarmy smile spreading across his lips. Ertide raised his cane in reply and ambled on.

The palace was packed with guests from all over his empire, but he saw far fewer of his family than he had expected. The Hostain dynasty was famed for its proliferation and there were branches all over the empire. His brother, Renshin commanded the Fourth Legion stationed at Rorash, and had four children of his own these days. He had not attended. His eldest sister, Fairlen governed Bresh over in the Ashlands, and she was famed for her love of a good party. Even as children, she was never so happy as when there was music and dancing. But Ertide supposed Bresh was a long way away, many weeks hard travel. Fairlen's eldest daughter, Fenlar was here, at least. Fenlar was a permanent fixture of the court in Celesgarde and Ertide half suspected she was also spying on things and reporting back to her mother.

Games on top of plots on top of schemes. If they only knew how little any of it mattered in the face of God's will.

A cheers went up as Ertide was walked into the grand hall. It was packed to the rafters with guests. Hundreds of faces all turned to see how infirm he had become. The whispers started soon after.

"The old king can't have long left."

"He hasn't named an heir yet."

"No wonder the barbarians have started raiding us again."

That last one was news to Ertide. If the savages from Aelegar were raiding empire lands again, it must have been kept from him on purpose. He was being forced out.

He limped through the crowd with Jertis on his arm, guiding him. Ylnaea appeared beside him, shooing Jertis away and taking Ertide's hand. She did not offer the same support, and Ertide soon found himself leaning more heavily on his cane.

"My king and husband, I'm so swelled with pleasure that you have chosen to appear," Ylnaea said as she guided him towards the throne.

Ertide mumbled some pleasantries about how he'd missed her of late, but they were vacant words and nothing more. They both knew she'd never warm his bed again, and that made her position precarious at best. She was queen, for now, but with no child to show for it, any power she had would vanish as soon as Ertide passed. If she was wise and cunning, as Ertide suspected she was, she'd already be gathering favours to herself.

Ertide mounted the steps and Jertis rushed forwards, helping Ylnaea lower him down into the cradle of the throne. White marble carved in the shape of overlapping angel wings. Even this, the seat of the Hostain power, the throne itself, was designed to remind everyone that the king ruled only by the grace of the angels and the will of God.

He looked out across the sea of faces. Family members, merchants, nobility, servants, bards, children, and interspersed throughout the people, towering over all those around them, angels. They were all waiting for him to speak. Ertide spotted Caran waiting at the foot of the steps. His youngest son was bedecked in the finest suit of black and gold Ertide had ever seen, and looked every part the prince. He was even wearing a feather pinned to his jacket, pearly white turning ember red towards the tip. An angel feather, gifted to him by none other than Eleseth, the Light Bringer. An obvious endorsement that none could miss.

Ertide tapped his cane against the stone floor and struggled to rise again. Jertis had to rush forwards and help him to his feet.

How far the Crimson Prince has fallen. Now a decrepit king.

"Thank you all for coming," Ertide said, glad his voice held out. "These celebrations of Prince Caran's birth are always my favourite time of the year. A time when the palace comes alive. When we welcome those from the furthest reaches of the empire. Family, friends, children of the God. We all come together in unity."

He paused for a moment, scanning the crowd. At the back, almost hidden behind a portly merchant woman, Ertide spotted Rikkan. His eldest son was wearing an exquisite military uniform. He had neither wife nor children beside him, but that was no surprise, they wanted nothing to do with him. It was rare to see Rikkan without a spear, but he had a sword buckled at his hip. It was often joked that no weapon had been forged that Rikkan could not slay a pack of wulfkin with, so broadly trained he was. As Ertide met his gaze, Rikkan sent a pointed glance sideways towards a tall angel with skin as dark as night. The Rider had made an appearance and was standing close to the door, his arms crossed over his robe, his pearly wings making him seem an imposing giant.

"The Sant Dien Empire has never been stronger," Ertide said, wondering how many people realised it was a lie. "Our enemies cower. Our poets and painters make works greater than ever before. And soon the fog of mystery will be burned away as we sail into the unknown and make the old world anew."

A thunderous round of applause shook the hall and Ertide waited it out, then gestured to his son. "And now a word from the man himself. My son, Prince Caran."

Caran mounted the steps quickly. He had the Hostain height and broad shoulders, but Caran had never been one for training with swords or shield. He'd left that to his eldest brother. He was soft around the belly and around the jowls, his dark skin pitted from illness as a child. Despite his softness, he moved with a grace and energy that was infectious. There were few who could stand in Caran's presence without joining him in regular smiles and laughter. He held a glass of red spice wine in each hand and offered one to Ertide as he turned to address the crowd.

"I can only hope I one day live up to my father's praise and his legacy."

He talks like I'm already gone.

"Our empire has always been strongest when we are closest to our allies," Caran continued, holding his glass up to the crowd. "Heaven's Light upon us all blesses us with a strength that no enemy can withstand. With a purpose that drives to always be better, to reach further and understand more. It is through the gracious bond with God and his children that we have such knowledge that places us as the greatest empire the world has ever seen. And it is time for the world to know it, too. As my father said, Heaven's Light will burn the fog away and bring civilisation to the old world."

He held his glass a little higher still and the crowd responded, holding up their own drinks. "To my father," Caran shouted. "To the Sant Dien Empire. To me, let's not forget it's my birthday." He grinned and laughed and a chuckle spread throughout the crowd. "And to God. Heaven's Light bless us all." He pulled the glass to his lips and drank, and the crowd drank with him.

"Let's celebrate!" Caran bellowed. The bards quickly took up the cue and within moments there was music and revelry such that Ertide almost felt alone with his son up on the dais.

Ertide stood frozen, the wine glass clutched in trembling hands. "That was masterful, son," he growled. "Almost sounded like a proclamation after accepting the crown."

If Caran caught the cold tone in his voice, he didn't show it. "We'll talk later, father. I must do the rounds and press some hands. Look after him, Jertis." He spun around and was gone, threading into the churning crowd within moments.

Ertide hated the way the celebration happened around him. As if he was one more statue lining the hall watching down on everyone with pitiless stone eyes. Many came to wish him well, promised to pray for his speedy recovery, but it was all lies. They didn't care if he recovered, they were all looking to who would be next to polish the throne with their kingly arse.

Caran moved through the hall like an eel through water, sliding easily from conversation to conversation, leaving beaming smiles and laughter in his wake. To the angels, he was courteous and deferential. To the merchants, he was suggestive and conspiratorial. To the nobility, he was charming and welcoming.

Rikkan, on the other hand, was standoffish to anyone who dared approach him. He preferred the company of soldiers, and had little to say to those who didn't look like they could wield a blade. They were night and day, his eldest and youngest sons.

His middle son, Welling, was already drunk and loudly boasting about the time he won the Nager Forest marathon. It was a dangerous run through the largest forest in the empire, and each year over half the participants never made it out, disappearing amidst the trees never to be seen again. Welling had entered on a particularly bad year when only two of two hundred runners made it out. Even then, he had actually come second. He'd never spoken of what he'd seen in the forest, but ever since that day, he'd been drowning himself in wine each evening, and sharp whip crack noises still sent him into paralytic shock.

Of his two daughters, there was no sign. Mertred was stationed in the Shadow Fort where she trained the next generation of soldiers to enter the legions. His eldest daughter had not relinquished any claim to the crown, but she deferred to her older brother in all things. She and Rikkan were both warriors at heart and though he was better with the sword, Mertred was the better commander.

Tristania, on the other hand, had long ago relinquished her claim to the throne. The last Ertide had heard, she was busy excavating some new ruins discovered over in the Ashlands. They were calling it the Temple of Dark Fire, and her last letter had been written in such a hastily scrawled hand, Ertide assumed his youngest daughter's excitement wouldn't let her sit still long enough to ride a carriage home. Tristania had always been like that, bubbling with energy and eager to use it to delve into the dark. He remembered how she used to squeeze behind wardrobes and under beds, always exploring. The servants had always hated being made to find her. It took them hours and she was always covered in dust and muck. Ertide smiled at the memory.

A raucous shout went up from a table at the far side of the hall. The twins were there with the Archangel. Even from a distance Ertide could tell what was happening. The Twins had cajoled Orphus into a drinking contest. Three ales a piece and the first to down all three was the winner. Ertide watched as the Archangel scooped up his second tankard and poured the contents into his helm. The ale disappeared into the darkness with a glugging noise. Even drinking and eating, none of the First Age angels showed any flesh, encased in their armour. Only their eyes showed, Orphus' sparkling blue as he cracked the tankard in a huge fist and reached for his third. Too late. Merian slammed her third empty mug on the table and raised her hands in victory with a whooping cheer. Orphus was next to finish, tossing his empty mug over his shoulder and batting it away with one of his wings. Emrik was the last to down his beer and gulped in a breath of air before belching it out again.

Merian was clearly gloating. She leapt to her feet, pointing at Orphus. The Archangel shook his head, blue eyes sparkling with laugher even in the darkness of his helm. Merian grabbed his gauntleted hands. Her own hands looked like a child's in his giant's grip. He stood and she tugged him out into the centre of the hall and danced to the merry tune the bards had strung up. He moved awkwardly opposite her, his armour clanking with each step.

Not to be outdone by his sister, Emrik launched himself up, and bowed to Eleseth. A few moments later, he had convinced the Herald of the Second Age, the most beautiful creature in existence, to dance with him. The twins cavorted about the hall, dancing, their angelic partners shining opposite them. If Rindon and Tresalla, Merian's husband and Emrik's wife, were put out at all by the twins' choices in partners, they didn't show it.

Ertide couldn't remember the last time he had felt so happy. To see so many of his family, his children and grandchildren, even his brothers and sisters, and so many others all enjoying themselves, seeming free of any care, it warmed him and eased the cold skeletal grip that had settled around his heart of late. He let himself be taken by the good cheer, buoyed up by it.

Until the Rider stopped by to pay his respects.

CHAPTER 14

"STILL CLINGING ON THERE, ERTIDE?" THE RIDER SAID, mounting the steps to the throne so he could stare down at him.

"Like a barnacle to a ship's hull. Speaking of which, you first boat is almost ready to launch, I hear. Keel tells me it's a vessel like no other."

The Rider scoffed. "Maybe it will be in another month. For now, it is nothing more than a few planks of wood strapped together by hopes and flaccid placations. At this rate, my fleet will take generations to build. It must be quicker."

Ertide leaned back in the throne and smiled up at the Herald of the Fourth Age. "It will always amaze me how those with unlimited time are the most likely to be irked by delay."

The Rider crossed his arms. "Don't spout your trite philosophical drivel to me, old man. I was born in the age of philosophy."

"So was I."

We are both creatures of the last age, yet here we are shaping this one.

Mathanial grinned. "An excellent point." He held out a large, calloused hand. "Will you walk with me, *King* Ertide Hostain?"

Ertide glanced over the hall once more. The twins still danced with their angelic partners. Emrik moved with a practiced grace as if he had been born to dance, while Merian swayed along to the music with the fluidity of a snake. Opposite them, the Archangel looked uncoordinated and awkward in his plate armour, moving as though he had no idea where to put his wings. Eleseth shuffled step to step, smiling so warmly and glowing like a forest fire at night. Neither of the twins were small, but they looked like drab children compared to their partners. And yet, despite Eleseth's radiant beauty and Orphus' shining strength, there was no doubt that the humans were the better dancers.

In two thousand years, you'd think they would have learned how to jig.

Ertide groaned as he started pushing to his feet. Jertis rushed forward to help, but the Rider held up a large hand to warn him back.

"Stop fawning over the old man and let him stand on his own feet," the Rider snarled. "If he can."

Ertide trembled, wobbled, and straightened up. He still had to look up to meet the Rider's gaze. "I can." He hoped the angel couldn't see how much it cost him.

The Rider led the way and the crowd of people parted before him like ice melting before a flame. Ertide followed, nodding some greetings here, spreading promises to talk later there. Mathanial led them away from the music and the dancing, towards the corner of the hall where the children were playing. Some with wooden swords, others with games, and some were sat around listening to a young, handsome woman telling scary stories of demons ruling the land before the angels came to free them all.

Rikkan shifted along the far wall, shadowing them, slipping along quiet and unnoticed. No one stopped him to trade pleasantries. Everyone knew there wasn't a drop of pleasantry in Ertide's oldest son. Ertide caught his gaze and gave a slow shake of his head. Whatever was happening here, it was not the time. They were not ready to make any moves.

Eventually the Rider stopped to stare down at a young boy playing with a puppy. They were wrestling and rolling in the straw, the dog barking, the boy squealing with delight. It was Murtan Hostain, Caran's oldest son, barely eight years old. The boy stopped and stood to something like attention when he noticed the Rider and the king looking down on him. The puppy had no such restraint and launched into the boy, knocking him to the floor. They were quickly wrestling again, their audience forgotten.

"I warned you this was coming, Ertide," the Rider said. He stood tall and strong, his arms crossed over his lithe chest, his dark skin radiating power. Beside him, Ertide was bent and broken and trembling, his own skin almost seeming grey. "It's time to name your heir."

"I will not abdicate my throne just because you tell me to, Rider. Whatever you think you are, you do not have that authority over me."

"I do. I speak with God's authority. I am his will made manifest."

"You are not!" Ertide turned to scowl up at the angel. "You're a spoilt child playing with fire, heedless of who is burned."

Mathanial turned sharply, looming over Ertide. Lightning crackled around the Rider's fingers.

Play the doddering king a while longer. Build Mathanial's ships, give him whatever he wants. Moon's words echoed through Ertide's mind.

Ertide raised a hand and softened his gaze. "I'm building your ships, Mathanial. As fast as I can. Diverting as many resources as able into their construction. I cannot change the time it will take. But I will not abdicate. Neither you, nor your father, have the right to order that."

The Rider's eyes narrowed as if he suspected a trap. "My father has the right to do anything he wishes, little king." He sighed, took a step back, and rubbed his fingers together until the lightning dissipated. "I don't wish to fight, old friend. I never wished to fight you. You can keep your throne and your title, old man. You don't need to abdicate. But you do need to name your heir. You need to step down. I insist."

Ertide laughed. "An abdication in all but name."

The Rider shook his head and had the gall to look sympathetic. "A reprieve of your duties. You have already started stepping back, take the final jump. Name your heir, hand over the responsibility to them. Keep the crown, keep the title, but spend what time you have left in graceful repose. It is time to let someone else rule, Ertide. Someone with less caution in their bones and more courage in their heart."

Ertide coughed and tasted blood on his lips. "A civilisation is lost, not when the messages of our heroes are forgotten, but when they are corrupted. When we are led by those with the loudest voices, rather than those with the keenest minds. When learning is ridiculed and ignorance lauded."

"More philosophical drivel, Ertide?" Mathanial said with an expansive sigh.

Ertide smiled up at the angel. "Just something my father once said. You'll get your wish, Mathanial. I'll name my heir at Springtide." That gave him a full month to make the decision and to delay. *A month for Moon to return.*

Mathanial laid a big hand on his shoulder and gave it a slight squeeze. The pressure was just a touch too tight to be comfortable. "It's the right choice, old man. Nobody can rule forever."

Except God?

After the angel left, Ertide found he had little taste for the frivolity of the celebration. Even watching his grandchildren dance and enjoying themselves had lost the shine. He slipped out of the great hall, shuffling along with Jertis just a few steps behind, ready to take his arm when he needed the help.

When. Not if. Ertide scoffed at his own dependence.

The great hall wasn't the only part of the palace full with noise and celebration. The guests were everywhere, in every hall and chamber and outside the grounds, too. They were only barred from the living quarters where the royal family stayed, and those areas were guarded by the men and women of the First Legion. Black armour with a single gold stripe across the chest plate, and something else, too. A red ribbon tied around the left arm. It was easy to overlook, but almost all the guards wore one.

Rikkan doing his job, singling out the soldiers he can trust. Ertide wondered how long before those who didn't wear the red were transferred to less comfortable posts as Rikkan filled the palace with his people.

He strolled into the gardens, his cane tapping a staccato beat as he shuffled along. The night was crisp, but not overly cold, and the clouds drifted in lazy patterns. Two of the three moons were up and bright; the Caped Moon's blue haze and the Bone Moon's bronze glare mixing into a ruddy light that made shadows appear deep and sinister. There were others about, some enjoying the flowers and statues and fountains, others enjoying the relative privacy and each other.

He passed a couple on a bench so lost in each other they didn't even notice him. She was an angel of the Fourth Age, her wings a silvery grey. He was a coiffed dandy with more rings in ears than wrinkles on his skin. His hand was in her robe, squeezing at her breasts, her's was down his britches squeezing at something else.

Nothing like a celebration to bring out the debauchery.

He shuffled past without a word. Ertide realised he so rarely came out to the gardens, and it was even more rare he took the time to stop and appreciate the beauty. He supposed that would be something he would have the opportunity for now. Time on his hands to do... nothing with. That was how things had been in the previous age, too. The Golden Age. Everyone had time to do nothing, to sit and think and be. So much had changed. Now it seemed everyone was always busy, him most of all.

"Sire," Jertis said softly. "Would you like me to fetch you a cloak or a glass of wine?"

Ertide shook his head. He realised he'd stopped before a fountain. Carved from marble, an angel stood atop a miniature fort, wings outstretched and hands raised to the sky. Water erupted up from the angel's hands and ran in clear rivers down his arms and face and clothes, pooling in the basin at the bottom. There, a trio of children, humans, were positioned with open buckets, collecting the water.

Even our art is to remind us from where our strength flows.

"Father? There you are," Caran called. Ertide glanced over his shoulder to see his youngest son hastening through the gardens, not even stopping to look at the beauty around him.

"Born in the Fourth Age," Ertide said quietly. Caran had been born the same year the Fourth Age began. He was only a few years older than his niece and nephew, the twins. All born in the Fourth Age, and all so busy all the time.

"I thought you'd gone off to bed before we could talk," Caran said as he reached Ertide's side. "Wine, Jertis."

Ertide nodded and Jertis hurried away. Ertide lowered himself onto the bench beside the fountain, using his cane as support. Caran stood before him, shifting from foot to foot.

Something tells me this won't be a pleasant conversation.

"Is this not quite the celebration, father?" Caran said. He took to pacing back and forth a few steps, all nervous energy. "I feel like the entire empire is celebrating with me. You don't see them doing that for any of my siblings."

Ertide kept silent, watching his youngest son. Some men struggled with silence.

"I saw you talking to Mathanial earlier," Caran said eventually.

"Ahh, so you've been conspiring with the Herald, have you?" Ertide said coldly. "Explains it."

"No! Of course not. I wouldn't call it a conspiracy. We've been talking. I... You know I've already taken over a lot of your duties, father. Meeting with Mathanial is just one of them. It turns out we have some... mutual opinions."

"Over who should take my crown?"

Caran opened his mouth to reply, then shut it. At least he had the respect to look abashed. Then his face crumpled and he shook his head, stopped pacing, and sat down next to Ertide.

"I know you don't love me like the others, father. Rikkan was your first and Mertred is more like you than you are. Even Welling, as insufferable as he is."

Ertide smiled and nodded. "He is."

Caran sighed. "God's Breath, father, you don't even deny it. I don't know what I ever did to make you hate me so."

"I don't hate you, son."

"You don't like me."

Ertide considered that. He thought about arguing. But it was true. He didn't much like Caran. He'd always tried to hide it, but now he supposed he must have done a poor job.

"I love you." That much was true. He loved all his children, even Caran.

His son snorted, shook his head, then sighed and straightened up. "Name me heir, father."

Ertide turned to look at his son. The man was strong, exuding calm even if he didn't feel it. "You're the youngest."

"True. But I was the one who sat at your knee while you ruled. I know all the stories, father. Mother told me all about her other children. Rikkan and Mertred were always off fighting. Welling could never pay attention long enough to sit still. And Tristania was always climbing anything with a handhold rather than learn to rule.

"I learned statecraft at your knee, father. I learned to rule by watching you. I went to all my classes. I even went to Arkenhold to study diplomacy. Did you know that, father? Did you know I went to university?"

Ertide looked away before his son could see his shame. He had not known. In truth, he had always paid so little attention to whatever Caran was doing. He had always seemed unimportant.

"Name me heir, father. Rikkan is the eldest, true, but he doesn't want the crown and he wouldn't know what to do with it. He is a blade, not a hammer, and right now we need to build, not kill."

"I was no different before I was crowned," Ertide said. "I had to learn. Rikkan will learn."

Caran shook his head sharply. "We both know the empire is in no state to give him the time. It cannot afford an unprepared ruler.

"Welling would piss the empire away. He is a fool and a sot and a coward."

"It's not your brother's fault he..."

"It *is* his fault, father. Do not try to absolve him of his fecklessness.

"Tristania wouldn't take the crown even if you offered it to her."

"You're forgetting Mertred, son. Your sister should be second in line."

Caran chuckled bitterly. "Oh no, father, I do not forget my sister. But let me say this plainly. If you choose Mertred as heir, our family will crumble. There'll be slaughter within a year. I will not call it war because the angels will not give us a chance to fight back. Within two years a new family will sit the throne, and in one hundred years no one will even remember the name Hostain. She will destroy us all, father."

"You don't think much of your sister."

Caran was silent for a moment, collecting himself. *The worst is still to come then.*

"I think she is like you, father. Too much like you. There is a rift formed between Heaven and empire, and you are the one who made it. You have carved a festering wound into us all, and each day the infection spreads."

Ertide felt the icy hands tightening around his heart again, squeezing the breath from his lungs. "Careful, son, you go too far."

The gravel scratched beneath his feet as Caran twisted off the bench and went down on one knee in front of Ertide.

"You know it's true, father. Your belligerence and defiance, your attempts to thwart Mathanial's orders. The empire is dying, and you're the one who's killing us."

"The angels are not the empire."

"But they are!" Caran shouted over him. He bowed his head rather than meet Ertide's anger. "They are, father. The Sant Dien Empire was built on the cooperation of Heaven and human, it is neither one nor the other, but both. The enemies we have crushed, the wonders we have built, the prosperity we have clawed from the earth, it is all by human and divine hands working together.

"You have undermined it, father, the very foundation of the empire. You are king. You set an example, and the example you have given us is one of open defiance at every turn. It is a sedition that will spread. IS spreading. Already there are people in Celesgarde refusing to go to morning prayers. They say the King walks the streets instead of praying, why shouldn't they? There are those who question the need for ships, for volunteers to explore. They are doubting the very animus of the age.

"All because of you, father."

Ertide sat stunned. He had not realised, but of course, he was king. People took notice of him. When he thought he was slipping out of a room unnoticed, there were always eyes watching him. When he shook his head at a proposal, there were those who took note, regardless of the words he eventually spoke. Caran was right, he had been openly seditious against heaven without even meaning to be. No wonder the Rider was so keen to be rid of him.

"Name me heir, father," Caran repeated. "Let me heal the wound you have sliced into the empire. Let me repair the rift between the crown and the divine. I have the angels' backing, they trust me. I know the economy better than anyone. The nobility trust me, the merchants respect me, and the people love me.

"I know I'm not the son you wanted. Not the warrior like Rikkan, the general like Mertred. I'm not as intrepid as Tristania, nor a loveable buffoon like Welling. But I'm the son you got, and I am the right choice. I am the king we need to save the empire and the family."

Ertide considered it, but really there was nothing to think about. Caran was right. A rift had formed, was growing, cracking its way down the alliance between heaven and empire, and left unchecked it would swallow them all whole. And Ertide was the cause. Caran was also correct, that he was the only sane choice for an heir, the only one who could knit the skin and let the body heal.

Without Moon, their conspiracy, their rebellion was dead before birth. And the longer the angel was away, the less likely it seemed he would return. Ertide could feel his death closing on him each day like wulfkin scenting blood. He had to do what was right for the empire and for his family.

Ertide nodded. "Springtide, son. We'll gather the whole family and I'll make the announcement then. You'll be king, Caran. I hope the crown sits easier on your head than it ever did on mine."

Caran shot to his feet, his smile beaming. He grabbed Ertide's hand and clutched it tightly. "It's the right choice, father. For the empire, for Heaven, and for the family."

Ertide smiled and nodded.

The right choice, yes, to bind ourselves to the divine for eternity. An eternity of grovelling at the angel's feet and bending to their every whim. Where are you, Moon?

CHAPTER 15

The month to Springtide passed in a blur of inflating agony to Ertide. His body was failing. The flesh seemed to burn from his bones and he couldn't summon the appetite to replace it. He couldn't feel his left arm at all anymore and each morning Jertis bound it in a sling hidden against his suit to give the impression he was simply holding it close against his chest. Walking across his rooms tired him out such that he needed to take a rest. Oronesus had sent him a chair with wheels attached so Jertis could move him about the palace. He didn't leave the palace anymore. Ertide did not want anyone to see him in such a condition. He looked a skeleton. A grey skeleton clinging to the last vestiges of a life burned out.

The pain was a constant thing. The icy claw poised around his heart never eased, only clutched tighter and tighter by the day. Every cough felt like something tearing inside, and there was always so much blood. Ertide was exhausted by the simple act of living.

Jertis wheeled him along hallways with bare stone floors. The servants had taken to removing the carpets to allow the chair easier access. Ertide had barely noticed. One day he woke, and all the carpets were simply gone. Who had made the decision and when was a mystery.

But that was no surprise. He was involved in so few of the decisions these days.

"The first of the Herald's ships is almost ready for launch," Jertis said as he pushed Ertide along. "A few more weeks, I hear, and they'll slide it out into the water. They say it can carry five hundred and horses and supplies, too. Five more are already under construction, and the Herald is pushing for the docks at Serinport to build them, also. Prince Caran claimed a fleet of twenty by year's end."

"Hmm," Ertide grunted. It had come to something that news of his empire came to his ears through his manservant.

Moon still hadn't appeared. He wasn't going to. Like always, the Apostle had vanished and when he might return was something no one could say. Ertide had always loved the flighty nature of his friend, but this time was different. This time it hurt. There were mere days until he would name Caran his heir. But more than that, Ertide could feel himself slipping, his health spiralling. He feared he would be long dead by the time Moon returned to himself and came back.

Every soldier they passed wore the crimson scarf around their left arm these days. Rikkan had been busy even as Ertide had been idle. Caran might be named heir, but the First Legion would forever be loyal to Rikkan. He hoped that wouldn't cause friction after he had gone.

"Here we are, sire," Jertis said. He pulled the chair to a halt, hurried forward and unlocked the study door, then pushed Ertide inside. Ertide waited impatiently until Jertis closed the door and pulled the blanket from his legs, then braced himself and helped pull Ertide out of the chair and to his feet. It was all so horribly undignified, but Ertide had learned the hard way to wait for help.

He ambled over to his desk, using his cane for support, and flopped down into the chair with a grateful sigh. All he'd done was cross the room, yet he felt the weight of the palace pressing down on him.

"What's this?" There were scrolls strewn across his desk, each one coiled and wrapped.

"Plans, sire," Jertis said as he rolled the wheeled chair away into the corner. "For the refurbishment of the Grand Samir courtyard."

"Oh, didn't we sort all that already?" He unrolled one of the scrolls to find a complex drawing of a wooden stage with hanging gardens, criss-crossing platforms, and a pond suspended in the centre so that visitors could walk underneath.

Father would have loved this. Testing the bounds of human ingenuity and creation for no sake other than beauty. A goal of the Third Age, now nothing but pointless frivolity.

"No, sire. The guild is still waiting for you to pick a design."

Ertide laughed. "Too old and weak to rule the empire, but here; pick where you want your pond." He unrolled another scroll and stared in wonder. "What would it need eight clocks for?" He pushed the scrolls to the side to be looked at more thoroughly another day.

"What's on the cards for today, Jertis?"

His servant smiled as he filled a glass with water and placed it on the desk. "Well, sire. Your family are beginning to arrive for Springtide. I'm sure they'll want to see you. General Mertred is due to enter the palace today. Her Sixth Legion camped outside overnight."

"She brought the entire legion?" Ertide grinned at the thought of a thousand soldiers camped outside the capital, probably scaring the crap out of Caran as if Mertred might consider a coup.

"In the mean time, I could set up the Clash board, sire?" Jertis said.

"Against you, Jertis? I'd have more of a challenge playing against my horse."

"Well, sire, you could always have a nap instead."

Ertide glared at the man, but he couldn't hold it. After a few moments, he was smiling, and then they were both chuckling. A year ago he could barely find time to scratch his arse, now the king was debating having a morning nap.

"Set up the board then."

They were ten moves into their second game of the morning and Jertis had already lost, even if he didn't know it yet, when a loud rapping at the door startled Ertide awake. He had to admit, he might have been dozing after all.

Jertis sprang from his chair and opened the door to Arandon waiting on the other side. Though Ertide had to admit he almost didn't recognise his grandson. He was weathered, all the fat burned from him, his cheeks chiselled and his belly no longer bulging. His hair was dusty and his skin had a look that said he had battled the elements. He was wearing riding leathers and there was dirt smudged over his jacket and mud caking his boots. Perhaps strangest of all, he didn't carry his little wooden board with all his notes.

"Arandon," Ertide said, grinning. He struggled, gripping hold of the table with his one good arm, and tried to stand. Jertis rushed to help. Ertide rounded his desk and grinned up at his grandson wondering when he gotten so tall. "What happened to you?"

Arandon frowned. "I could ask the same, Grandfather. I wasn't gone so long, was I?"

"Ha! You think this is sudden? Try living with it. It feels like only yesterday I was teaching your father how to swing a sword. Now I struggle to wield my cane. Come in. Sit. Wine?"

They sat while Jertis poured wine. Arandon said nothing, yet his gaze never left Ertide. "So where have you been?"

"The Ice Isles, Grandfather. I left word before I departed." He turned to Jertis who only nodded in reply. "It was... quite the experience."

Ertide nodded along. "But why? The negotiations over leviathan oil weren't so important."

Arandon took a sip of wine, followed by a gulp. Then he turned to Jertis. "You can leave now."

The servant hesitated, but Ertide waved him away and he slipped from the study out into the hall. Arandon waited until he was gone.

"What's all this about, then?" Ertide asked impatiently.

"Do you remember what we were looking for before I left?" Arandon asked. "Before you fell ill."

Ertide nodded. "The truth. Tarkum Chaim and..."

"The Knights Exemplar. The war after God and the angels and the Exemplars fought back the demons. A war fought between the demons and the Shattering."

Ertide remembered now. It had seemed so important at the time, deciphering his father's mad notes in the book.

"You said: *History is mutable, written not by the hand of relevance, but instead by those with ink to spare.* It got me thinking, Grandfather. If our true history is hidden, changed, what about others who keep history? What about the Lorekeepers?"

Ertide laughed. "They dance around heresy, Arandon. You think they keep the truth while we drown in lies?"

"I did. I do." Arandon leaned forward. "I went to see the Ice Walker who was here to negotiate, and she showed me some of her tattoos. Just a glimpse, but there was truth there we do not have in our books. More, she claimed she only kept a part of our shared history. All Lorekeepers only keep part. Each one is a living, breathing, walking tome, but we need dozens of books to tell the truth of thousands of years of history. So I accompanied her back to the Ice Isles."

Arandon shook his head, his eyes wide. "The isles are like a different world, Grandfather. They live in huts, great and small. They move each day, isle to isle, only stopping at night. They fish and sail and hunt. They do not worship God or the angels. At first they claimed not to worship anything, but I stayed with them for weeks. Eventually I learned the truth. They worship the ice, Grandfather. And they worship the Lords Beneath the Ice."

Ertide shook his head, sitting back. This was no longer just dancing around heresy. It was blatant and enough to see them hanged, even him, king or no. "They worship demons? Dead demons. The Lords Beneath the Ice were all killed during the Shattering, when the ice broke apart and the demons poured from the depths."

Arandon smiled wide, his dark eyes glinting. "Would you like to know the truth, Grandfather? Everything I learned. Everything I pieced together. Shall I tell you what Heaven has hidden from us?"

Ertide thought about it. He was already neck deep in heresy with his plots with Rikkan and Moon, not that they were coming to anything. More than that, he was already dying. Besides, he wanted to know.

"Tell me."

Arandon leaned back, his smile vanishing. "I want something in return. I want in."

"In?"

"To your inner circle. To whatever you and my father have planned. Don't try to deny it, I'm not a fool. I can help, Grandfather. I want to help. So let me in."

Every person they added to the conspiracy was another step towards making it irrevocable. Another person in danger, and another avenue for the sedition to be uncovered. And Moon had said not to trust Rikkan's children. But Moon was often the first to admit he didn't know everything. His seer's sight was imperfect, seeing around events rather than the heart of them. Ertide had already considered all his options. Soon, he would have to gather his allies, reveal the truth to them to bind them to the cause. *If* he was still planning to go ahead with it. It was all pointless without Moon though. Without the Apostle, they had no way to kill an angel, no chance of taking their blood. Without Moon, Ertide was dead. The only choice was, did he take more of his family with him?

"I could order you to tell me," Ertide said.

"I would refuse."

The iron in his grandson's voice surprised him. "You would refuse an order from your king?"

Arandon was silent a moment, considering carefully. "This order. Yes. This is a trade or nothing."

Whatever happened to him out on the ice tempered him. The soft boy is gone. Here sits a real Hostain, some of his father showing in his spine.

Ertide busied himself re-setting the Clash board, then sat back and waved at it. Arandon scooted forward and made his first move. As they played, Ertide told him everything. What Moon had said, what he claimed angel blood could do, how they had brought Rikkan over to their cause, and the steps the three of them were making. Arandon listened and moved his pieces.

"Now you know," Ertide said as he slid his angel piece across the board and captured the sixth Shrine, ensuring his victory. "Now you're *in*, even if you would prefer not to be."

Arandon nodded as he worked, resetting the board again. It was customary to spin it around when a match was finished so the players could battle again from the other side, with the pieces of darkness instead of light. But Arandon didn't bother. He immediately moved his Reaver piece towards the centre of the board. A bold and dangerous gambit.

"Have you ever heard of the Exodus, Grandfather?"

Ertide moved his own piece and shook his head.

"Neither had I. Not in any of the divine texts, and not in any history books. But the Lorekeepers know all about it. They have entire keepers whose bodies are covered in the trials we all faced. You see, we're not from here, Grandfather, not originally. Humans, all of us, came from across the sea, on ships as big as the Rider wants us to build now. Grander, even. Giant boats capable of carrying entire cities worth of us. We were fleeing something, not in tens or hundreds, but in our thousands, we boarded our ships and fled across the ocean.

"Not many of those ships made it. Some lost at sea, others pulled down into the darkness by the things chasing us. But eventually those of us who did survive made it here. To the lands we now call the Sant Dien Empire, the Ice Isles, the Ashlands, even Aelegar. We spread out across it, this newly abundant land."

Arandon moved a pack of wulfkin onto the flank where they were threatening Ertide's last Knight Exemplar. It was a mismatch of power, but Ertide had his pegasus ready to swoop in and carry the Exemplar to safety.

"This is where our own history books pick up. We didn't realise this land already had occupants." Arandon looked up from the board, his gaze measuring. "Demons." He paused, waiting as if expecting Ertide to say something.

"What I found particularly interesting is this; the Lorekeeper's tattoos don't mention demons. Not once. They go into great detail about the Lords Beneath the Ice, the Malevolence, the Ghostfires, the Sin Eater. And Tarkum Chaim."

Ertide paused, his hand held above the board. Arandon had somehow put both his Exemplar and his hawk in peril. He couldn't save both. "What is Tarkum Chaim?"

"The Soul Reaver," Arandon said, a wary smile on his lips. He shook his head. "Terror. He rode a bone chariot across the sky, pulled by skeletal horses. Every time our three moons shared the sky, he would ride out and reap the souls of anyone he found. Not killing them. Binding them to his deviant torture for eternity."

Ertide snorted. "A ghost story to scare children."

"Is it?" Arandon asked. "Then why is Tarkum Chaim in the book, Grandfather?"

Ertide was losing. Arandon had claimed the centre of the board and had built a fortress of pieces there, sending them out to secure shrines.

"Tarkum Chaim is real, Grandfather. Or was real. Sometime between the end of the supposed demon war and the Shattering, God went to war with Tarkum Chaim. Given that God is still here and the Soul Reaver is not, we can guess who won."

Ertide leaned back in his chair, his eyes on the board, but his mind elsewhere. "Supposed demon war?"

"Well, that's the really interesting thing, Grandfather. The Lorekeepers never mention demons. The Lords Beneath the Ice, the Soul Reaver, all the others they do mention predate the Exodus." He paused, looking expectant.

One by one, Ertide pushed his remaining pieces over, signifying his surrender of the game. "They predate the Exodus. Which means they predate our coming here. God and his angels only appeared to us towards the end of the First Age, the start of the demon war and by then we'd already been enslaved for generations." He shook his head as if he could make all the pieces of the story fall into place. "You're saying these things, Tarkum Chaim, the Malevolence predate God."

Arandon was nodding slowly. "Or at least our introduction to him."

Ertide pushed over the last of his pieces. "But if the Lorekeepers don't mention demons at all... Is the Soul Reaver and the others the demons then? Those who enslaved us?"

"Tarkum Chaim takes souls, not people, Grandfather. Or so all the Lorekeepers agree."

"It doesn't matter," Ertide said. "The book says God went to war with Tarkum Chaim after the demon war. And the Lords Beneath the Ice were fought during the Shattering. So, who were the demons?"

Arandon sat there, grinning like a cat with three fish, waiting.

Ertide moved his mouth, tried to force the words out, but they wouldn't come. It upset everything he had been taught to believe his entire life. It changed everything.

"It was us," he said. "We were the demons."

Arandon nodded again. "It was never a war to free us, Grandfather. God sent his children to pacify us. And he won."

Ertide couldn't help the laugh that burst from his lips. It was born of madness, of incredulity. Of hope.

"This is it, Arandon. This is exactly what I need. To bind someone entirely to a cause, use three anchors: Greed. Fear. Anger. This is the final anchor. With this I will bind our allies to us with chains even God cannot break."

And it will still all be for naught unless Moon tells us how to kill them.

CHAPTER 16

The morning of Springtide came too quickly. The shortest day and the turning point of the entire year. A day when every prayer was aimed towards the future, begging the God for bountiful harvests and fat children and all those other good things.

Ertide stood at the balcony window of his King's Shrine, trembling from the effort and from the chill of the wind gusting in, tracing icy tendrils across his skin. Across Celesgarde, bells rang, signalling the end of morning prayers. He snorted. He hadn't prayed in weeks, longer even. Ylnaea no longer visited him, nor forced him to kneel with her. Ever since his failing had become apparent, no one seemed to care at all whether the dying king said his prayers. They were all looking to the next generation. They were all chasing Caran around now.

He stared out across the city to the beam of light that was always visible no matter the time of day or distance from the source. Heaven's light. Ertide still bristled every time he thought of it. What the God had done was genius in a diabolical way. He had sent his angels to pacify the most violent of humanity, then made mythological monsters of any who dared to resist, naming them demons. He had built an entire religion around the worship of him, and had slowly changed all mention of things ever being otherwise. Two thousand years since the end of the First Age, and their true history was lost. Only the Lorekeepers still remembered and they were renowned for being fiercely jealous of their wisdom. Yet, Arandon had convinced them to give up their secrets.

The question Ertide kept returning to was: did any of it really matter? Humanity had been conquered, subjugated. But it was not as though the God had not accomplished good things for their benefit. He had fought against the old enemies, Tarkum Chaim and the Lords Beneath the Ice. God had won. Nobody had heard of those old terrors for thousands of years.

God had brought humanity knowledge and culture, peace and prosperity. He had ushered them through a dark time and into a golden age where they had built such wonders as the temple at God's End, the Seven Spires of Felbrek, the shining city of Hope. What right did Ertide have to defy all of that?

Mine is a rebellion two thousand years too late.

All his deliberation was pointless anyway. He stared out across his city and wished to see dark wings flitting through the sky. If anyone could make sense of it all, it would be Moon. The past, present, and future were all his to see.

But doesn't that mean he knew the truth all along and was hiding it from me?

A knock at the door and Jertis' voice, soft through the wood. "Sire, do you need my help?"

Ertide spent a few more seconds glaring out towards Heaven's light, then closed his window.

The palace was full of Hostains. They were a large family with many little offshoots and branch families. All had turned up to witness Caran's naming as heir. Ertide found he had cousins he didn't remember, nieces and nephews he never knew he had, and more grand nieces and nephews than he could bother learning their names. They all looked at him with pity, and he hated it. They all curried favour with Caran, and Ertide hated that even more.

He had until the evening to the official ceremony and found little patience with which to sit around the palace. Nor would he hide away in his study like a timid recluse. Instead he had Jertis wheel him around in his chair, through gardens white and purple with new bloom, and out past the arboretum. When they came to the stables, he ordered Jertis to stop.

Ertide loved the stables. It was always noisy, but a warm, welcoming noise. Horses braying, dogs barking, even the occasional piercing cry of a hawk. The stalls were full to bursting now with so many visitors and the stable hands were hard at it.

There were three large paddocks attached to the stables. The first had a trio of horses charging around, getting some exercise. The second housed a single pegasus, gleaming white with wings so large it seemed they could blot out the sky. The beast was happily eating at a trough, its tail swishing back and forth. No saddle on that creature. Pegasi were too proud to allow saddles, and the Rider himself warned that none could mount one without his express permission. To date, that meant no human had ever ridden a pegasus.

In the third paddock, Merian held loosely to a small black pony's reins and was trotting it about the enclosure. Her daughter Urtrid was on the horse's back, grinning from ear to ear. Merian had always loved to ride, and it seemed her passion was as strong in her young daughter as it ever had been in her.

Ertide watched for a few minutes until Merian spotted him. She smiled and trotted the pony over to the fence.

"Grandfather, it's good to see you out and about."

"Ish akin! Ish akin!" Urtrid shouted, bouncing up and down in the saddle.

Merian smiled. "Calm down, Peanut. Think about it before you say it."

The little girl frowned dramatically. "It's the king," she said slowly.

"He is," Merian said.

"I am," Ertide agreed. "For a while yet hopefully."

Merian reached up and stroked her daughter's hair. "She gets very excited and rushes over her words. Sometimes I think her little mind runs five times as fast as her mouth."

Urtrid stuck her tongue out at her mother, then broke into a fit of giggles.

"Better that than her mouth running faster than her mind," Ertide said. "That's how we ended up with your uncle Welling."

Urtrid giggled some more. "Welling's a drunk."

Merian's dark cheeks flushed. Ertide only laughed.

"Sorry, Grandfather," Merian said. "Children have a habit of repeating things they shouldn't even remember." She sent a playful slap at her daughter who just kept giggling. Merian then waved over a waiting stable hand and let them take the pony and her daughter away to continue her lesson.

"A passion for riding, you must be pleased," Ertide said.

"You have no idea," Merian said. "Until last month, she was absolutely terrified of horses. I was starting to think I birthed the wrong child."

Ertide chuckled and leaned back in his chair to watch Urtrid trotting her pony around the paddock.

Merian leaned on the fence, peering at him. "You seem distracted, Grandfather."

He nodded. "I have a lot on my mind."

"So why are you chatting to a wastrel like me? Shouldn't you be talking to the angels or to uncle Caran?"

"Sometimes I find, when I have a big decision to make, talking to people about unimportant things can help."

"Ah," Merian sketched a dramatic bow. "I'm nothing if not unimportant."

Ertide grinned and nodded. "A wastrel, you might say. Almost as bad as your twin."

"So what's the big decision? Something about the whole heir thing?"

Ertide stayed silent and slowly tilted his head to look up at Jertis. The man caught the hint immediately and coughed politely.

"I'll go fetch you another blanket for your legs, sire. Wouldn't want you to get cold." He bowed, then strode away towards the stables. He'd wait there until he was needed again.

"You have him remarkably well trained, Grandfather. I might have to take some notes."

Ertide chuckled and threw aside his blanket. "I'd be lost without

Jertis." He leaned on his cane and struggled out of his chair, stumbling the two steps until he was leaning on the fence. Just that small effort left him out of breath. Merian eyed him warily, but didn't offer to help. He was grateful for that and so very sick of people offering him their help.

"I'm trying to decide whether to take the empire to war." It was almost the truth.

"Oh," Merian turned and leaned back against the fence, watching her daughter trot about on the pony. "With Aelegar again?"

Ertide stayed silent.

"Well, you know I've never been to war, Grandfather. I like to play with my sword and shield just like the others. Very little beats a good work out on the sparring grounds, but I've heard your and father's stories. War always sounds... pretty bad."

Ertide laughed at that. "A resounding understatement. It is bad. Always bad."

"So, I guess you need to ask yourself whether the potential good you might accomplish with this war, will outweigh the bad you'll definitely cause. Sorry, that's a childish way of looking at it."

Ertide shook his head. "That might be the wisest thing you've ever said."

"The competition is not fierce." Merian grinned over her shoulder at him.

"Perhaps I should name you heir."

Merian scoffed. "Oh, please Heaven no, Grandfather. I don't want your crown."

"No?"

"No! It wouldn't suit me at all. And I hope you don't mind me saying so, Grandfather, but I don't think it suits you very well either." She opened her mouth as if to say more, but shut it again. "Sorry. Not my place."

Ertide trembled as he leaned against the fence. It was a lot of effort just to remain standing. "Go on. Speak your mind."

Merian tapped her foot absently against the dusty ground, then spun about to stare at Ertide. "For as long as I can remember, I've heard stories of you, your exploits. Father used to regale us. He spoke of you with such reverence. *A titan of battle, a master strategist, a steel with no bend and no break.* I've heard the same from others, too. They always said you had such passion. For battle, for the empire, for the family. I..." She paused, stared at him, shook her head. "I don't see it. That fire that must have burned through your veins is extinguished. And I can't but wonder, is it age that dulled your sword or disuse?

"I'm no warrior like you or my father. I can hold my own well enough, but they'll never name me master swordsman. God's Breath, I don't want them to. But I do yearn for adventure, to stamp my name on this world in some way.

"I have seen the way the crown has made you smaller, Grandfather. How heavy it must be. I fear it would do the same to me, crush me into a shape I do not want. So, no. I don't want it."

Ertide let his cane fall and laid his hand on top of Merian's there on the fence. "That passion you have, that drive for greatness. It is the Hostain blood in you, Granddaughter. All the most memorable of our family have it. And I pity those who do not. I pity your brother."

"Emrik?" Merian scoffed. "Don't pity him, Grandfather. My brother will do something great. Something... He will be remembered. He just needs to figure out what. I promise you, once he finds his passion there will be no stopping him. He excels at anything he tries his hand at, but bores so easily. But once he finds it, that thing that lights a fire in his veins, that whips his flanks driving him to be better. Once he finds that, he will be the best of us."

Ertide squeezed her hand. She had such trust in her twin, such belief. He wondered if she saw something in Emrik he did not.

"And what about you, Granddaughter? What do *you* want?"

"Adventure. To travel east to west and see what there is beyond our borders. To ride and breed horses. I suppose I share some of the Herald's values in that way. I admit, I've always envied Mathanial somewhat.

"I want to see my brother find his passion. To raise my daughter to be even better than me." She spun about and threw her hand towards the second paddock. "Oh, and I *really* want to ride a bloody pegasus."

"Ahh," Ertide grinned. "There will be your road to greatness, Merian. You will be the first of us to ride a pegasus. If any of us can do it, it's you. Tame one of the beasts whether the Rider wills it or not."

As if sensing the intent, the pegasus raised its head and snorted. It stomped its great hooves twice, then spread its glorious wings. With a short canter, and a few thunderous beats, the pegasus launched into the air, a cloud of dust billowing beneath it. It brayed as it turned, flying back over the stables then up into the sky and across the city.

Merian sighed. "Now that would make me happy, Grandfather."

CHAPTER 17

Ertide sat in the throne room while dozens of family members drifted in. He'd wanted a polite gathering, a small affair, but what he'd gotten was anything but.

Servants spread around the walls waiting for summons. Three grand tables lined the hall, each one bustling with roast hog, loaves of fresh baked bread, baskets of fruit, dipping pastries, gravy ponds, crackling duck, ale and mead and wine. Springtide starting early.

There were already a few angels in attendance. Orphus, the Archangel, stood with the twins, towering over them in his golden armour. Whatever he had said must have been funny, because Emrik was roaring.

Eleseth, the Light Bearer, sat by the grand hearth with a gaggle of children most of whom Ertide couldn't name, but he assumed they were all relatives. Some of the children grinned, others looked shocked or rapt. Eleseth had always been a good storyteller.

Oronesus, the Bookkeeper stood by the doorway, an expansive leather-bound tome floating before her. She was jotting down names of all those who attended, keeping a record for posterity. A new heir was about to be named, after all. The next step in the Fourth Age was about to be taken. It was an event that would go down in the history books, and Ertide expected those books would be written by angels.

Of course, Mathanial was also in attendance. The Rider, the Herald of the Fourth Age, would not miss this spectacle. For so long he had wanted someone else, someone more compliant to take Ertide's place on the throne. Now he was getting it. Everything he wanted. His ships were being built, Caran would do whatever he asked with the power of the crown. Even knowing the truth of the First Age, Ertide could do nothing without Moon.

Such impotence. Once I was grand, I was mighty. I was young and healthy.

He remembered well the day when he was named Terin Hostain's heir. It hadn't been anything like this, surrounded by family members. No. He had recently returned from the siege of Fort Dieshel. Barbarians from Aelegar had swam across the Flooded Vale under the cover of night and flotsam. They'd scaled the walls of the fort and silenced the sentries, then slaughtered half the garrison in their beds. The other half were taken as thralls, never to be seen again. Men and women of the empire just gone. The angel stationed at the fort was a warrior of the First Age, Mihiriel, the Shining Spear. By his own account, he had slain almost one hundred of the barbarians. But then he had fled, leaving the fort to be captured. Ertide had never understood that. Why hadn't Mihiriel stayed? If the angels were as invulnerable as they claimed, he could have defended the fort all by himself.

I'm missing something. A vulnerability. The secret Moon was supposed to bring back with him.

Ertide was younger than the twins at the time, but he was full of fire. The Crimson Prince, they called him, and he loved it. He lived up to the name. He'd ridden out with a full legion of one thousand soldiers. Two angels flanked him from the sky, both mighty warriors from the First Age clad in impenetrable armour. They'd crashed upon the fort like a wave against a cliff. The walls of Dieshel were thick and strong and the gate many times reinforced. Ertide lost almost a hundred soldiers in that first foolish attack. The barbarians had laughed and thrown stones, pulled up their furs and bared their arses, squeezing out turds from the top of the walls. Such vulgar mockery. Ertide had pulled back, defeated, and turned his eyes upward towards the angels, neither of whom had joined the battle.

For three days the siege went on. Each assault on the walls was rebuffed. A few of the barbarians were killed each time, but more of the empire's soldiers died throwing themselves at the gates. And still the angels stayed back, watching from the skies but not taking part. Ertide couldn't understand it. His soldiers, his people were dying on the field of battle while the angels watched and did nothing. They were of the First Age, born for battle, each one a warrior with irresistible strength and devastating power. Yet they would not help.

On the third day, Ertide had gone to the angels and asked for aid. It was Selitha, the Star Hammer, a tall angel with green armour to match her emerald stare, who answered. She had simply said they would join the battle when the time was right. There was no arguing with her. There was never any arguing with an angel. But Ertide thought that was the first time his faith had been tested and found wanting. When his soldiers were dying because the angels refused to fight. He'd been so angry that he sat in his tent cursing their names in a rage. And God had not smote him for it. That was the day his rebellion had been born. For so long a rebellion of one.

He broke the siege that very night, sending the bulk of his legion against the walls once more, while Ertide himself along with twenty of his best soldiers used the barbarian's own tactic against them, swimming through the waters around the fort and scaling the walls on the far side. It had been a bloody, pitched battle through the fort to the gate, and Ertide lost fifteen of his twenty, but they threw open the gate and his legion poured through. Only then had the angels deigned to join the battle. Selitha crashed from the sky like the falling star she was named for. Her hammer cracked the earth and the barbarians fell before her. It was all the proof Ertide had needed that the angels could have taken the fort at any time.

When he returned to Celesgarde, he was hailed as a hero. The Crimson Prince returned victorious over the barbarians again. The people of his city swarmed around him and his surviving soldiers, cheering for a battle they knew nothing about. His father had ridden out to meet him, and there on the streets of Celesgarde, surrounded by soldiers and by citizens of the empire, Terin Hostain had raised his voice to a shout and named Ertide his heir. There was no pomp, no ceremony. No angel supervision.

Did my father do that on purpose? Name me heir in so public a way so the angels could not deny it or argue against it? I always thought you weak, father, a puppet. Now I think you fought back as well as you could. You pinned your hopes on me, and I have failed you.

So many of Ertide's family crowded the hall now. They had flocked from all over the empire to see Caran named heir. There was Renshin, Ertide's younger brother and commander of Rorash in the southern mountain passes. He was a bull of a man as wide as he was tall, and loud enough Ertide used to tease him his father was actually a fog horn. He already had a leg of duck in one hand and a jack of ale in the other, and was regaling their sister Ellian with some story. She looked bored, but Ellian was no warrior, she was a priest.

Rikkan stood apart, as he always did, ghosting around the edges of the hall. No one dared approach him. Ertide's oldest son was never well liked even by his own family. Even his own children hated him.

Welling was already drunk, all bleary eyes and sudden silences. He was sat with his aunt Delia, a scalpel of woman, and two of his cousins who were matching him drink for drink as if Springtide was already well under way.

Mertred, Ertide's first daughter, sat with her two sons. They were men grown now, and soldiers serving under their mother in the Shadow Fort. Mertred was tall and bluff, her skin dark as old wood. She was dressed in her uniform, gold on black, and had her sword laid across the table. She met Ertide's eyes and gave her father a nod. He nodded back. He'd always loved Mertred, but Caran was right. She was so much like her father, and her discomfort around the angels was all too evident for anyone to see.

Even Tristania, Ertide's youngest, had turned up for the event. She was beaming, a crowd of aunts and uncles, nieces and nephews, cousins and those even further removed, gathered around her as she told some tale of adventure. There was never a dull moment with Tristania around and her joy could light up a room.

And then there was Caran, soon to be heir to the throne, and already all but running the empire. He hovered near the foot of the throne, warmly greeting anyone who came close, but never venturing too far as if Ertide could somehow forget his presence. He had dressed in resplendent red with black trimming and his jacket was festooned with artful buckles and brass buttons and almost trailed to the floor. He'd even strapped a sword to his hip, though Ertide knew his youngest son had no idea how to use it. But it was about the image. It looked good for the prince heir to be armed.

"Grandfather," Arandon whispered as he bent down and touched Ertide's arm. He was standing beside the throne, his note board grasped in one hand, a pencil in the other. Taking notes, making an account of the event separate from the one Oronesus took.

How will the two accounts differ, I wonder?

"Is everyone here?" Ertide asked.

Arandon sent a glance across the hall. "Everyone who matters."

"Best get on with it then."

"Unless you would prefer to call the whole thing off?"

Ertide glanced up at Arandon who smiled slightly, bowed his head a little and stepped down the stairs away from the throne to wait with the rest of the crowd of family members.

Ertide swept his gaze over them all one last time. Over a hundred Hostains across four generations. From children to adults to elders. His family. His blood.

Ertide slammed his cane down on the stone dais three times to signal it was time to get the farce underway. As the crowd of waiting family guttered into silence, Jertis crept forwards and helped Ertide stand. Some things were better done on his feet, the last gasp of his dignity.

"Thank you all for coming," he said loudly. At least his voice hadn't failed him yet, though breathing too deeply made the icy claws clutch at his heart a little tighter. "Any chance for a good meal and some ale with family, eh?" He chuckled and a wave of laughter and appreciation rippled through the crowd of family members.

"So many faces here I recognise," Ertide continued. "And just as many I don't. I'm sorry about that. I wish I'd spent more time getting to know you all. But ours is a broad family. A tree with roots as deep as the world, and more branches than rivers feeding the World Vein. The

Hostain blood runs strong in us all. The blood of the Saint, who forged humanity into an empire. The blood of rulers, who have held us all together and brought us prosperity and wisdom and strength."

His words bordered on heresy, but didn't quite slip over. The angels would do nothing if he did not speak out against God.

"The blood of my grandfather, Ekart Hostain, who first brokered peace with our now Ice Walker allies. The blood of my father, Terrin Hostain, who laid the foundations for Etrinlow, Colberra, Salt, and a dozen other cities across the Sant Dien Empire.

"And my blood." Ertide paused, let his gaze go distant.

What have I achieved? A few battles fought and won? A peace with Aelegar they break whenever they please? A simmering tension between Heaven and empire that might yet see us all crushed? What will my legacy be?

A cough brought him out of his reverie, and he noticed a few furtive glances. He'd been quiet for too long. They probably thought his mind weak. His family finally seeing the crumbling ruin he had become.

He drew in a breath to continue and a coughing fit hit him. He sank back onto the throne, holding a handkerchief to his mouth and coughing into it. Jertis was at his side in a moment, fussing. Ertide forced control of himself and swallowed down the pain. He took a goblet of wine from Jertis and gulped greedily, then shoved it back into the man's hands and waved him away. The handkerchief was wet and sticky with blood and Ertide pocketed it quickly.

"My time is coming to an end," he said loudly to the murmuring crowd of his family. "In more ways than one. So it's time I named my heir, to act as regent from now until I pass."

He sought out his children. Rikkan stood alone, cold and rigid. Ever the warrior, always ready to fight, but caring of little else.

Mertred, the general, sat with her soldier sons, the concern clear on her face. She who would lead the empire to its ruin, breaking before she would bend.

Welling was a wastrel, too damaged by what he had seen in the forest to be of any use to anyone.

Caran, a born politician and leader, smiling broadly from the foot of the throne. He who would heal the empire and be the bridge between Heaven and crown.

And Tristania, the flighty adventurer who hated responsibility.

He'd stalled long enough, hoping Moon would appear, a last second interruption because the angel loved his drama. But he wasn't coming and that meant Ertide had no choice. Except he hated having no choice. He hated being backed up against the wall. He hated being told what he had to do. He was king, ruler of the Sant Dien Empire for a little longer at least. The King did not answer to Heaven.

Time to do something unexpected.

"As my heir and regent to the throne," Ertide said loudly. Caran started up the steps, grinning. "I name my grandson Arandon Hostain."

The throne room erupted into noise. Some shouted objections, others their support. The angels sent sharp glances between each other, but it was too late. The decision had been made, too publicly to be renounced.

Across the hall, Rikkan smiled briefly, then ducked out of the door-way. Gone. Mertred was uncharacteristically silent, her narrowed eyes locked on her father. Welling and Tristania were both cheering like it was either the best news they'd ever heard, or the funniest jest.

Caran, though, had stopped, one foot on the steps. His smile had frozen, gone cold. His eyes were pits of anguish and fury. Ertide gave him a sorry smile and wished he could explain, but he couldn't, and Caran would never listen anyway. He would only ever see the injustice of it.

Arandon brushed past his frozen uncle as he mounted the steps. Though they had not planned it, he did not look surprised. Rather, he gave Ertide a knowing nod as if he had seen the play coming like a gambit in Clash.

Too sharp for his own good.

"There'll be no living with the little shit now," Emrik called from across the hall.

Merian laughed along with her twin. "That's King Little Shit, brother."

Both twins clapped. If either of them had any misgivings about it, they didn't show it. By usual convention, Rikkan would have been heir, and Emrik his heir. But Emrik continued to have no ambition.

Arandon reached the top of the steps and turned to stand next to Ertide. He glanced down and Ertide gave him a nod.

"I know this is unexpected," Arandon said, trying to pitch his voice to carry over the rumbling crowd.

"Why father?" Caran screeched from the bottom step. "What did I do? Why do you hate me so?"

Renshin was up in a flash, far quicker than most would think possible given his size. He crossed the distance and grabbed Caran around the shoulders, pulling him close. "Bit too much to drink there, nephew."

"Get off me, you pig." Caran sent an elbow into Renshin's gut, but he might as well have assaulted an iron door for all the give in Renshin's chest.

"I think not, lad. Let's get you out of here before you embarrass yourself before the new king, eh?" He held Caran tight as he dragged him on, steering them towards the exit. "Wonderful shindig as always, brother. Quite the surprise, eh?" He laughed as he pulled the struggling Caran away.

The rest of Arandon's improvised speech went quickly. He was not the orator that Caran usually was, and nor did he have the force of personality of either of the twins, but he was calm and confident. He promised to further the impetus of the age, bring prosperity to the Sant Dien Empire, and build new levels of trust between Heaven and crown. He said everything the angels needed to hear.

CHAPTER 18

JERTIS WHEELED ERTIDE BACK TO HIS QUARTERS. IT WAS FAR from late, but Ertide found himself tired so quickly these days. And besides, the day was no longer about him, but about Arandon. Word had spread of the surprise announcement and soon Arandon found himself swamped with well-wishers, admirers, hangers on, and those simply begging favour. He'd have to get used to it soon, but Ertide wondered if he would come to love or despise the constant attention.

Springtide was well under way now with singing and dancing on the streets of Celesgarde. Pyres were lit in many of the town squares and prayers and sacrifices were offered to the God to beg for a good harvest. All part of the ritual of worship. Night might have fallen on the shortest day, but the dawn would bring a new start, the beginning of a season of growth.

No one had seen Caran since Renshin dragged him out of the throne room. He'd stormed off in a huff and vanished. Ertide hoped he'd find peace with the decision. He'd never meant to hurt his youngest, but he could not allow him to sit the throne. Not after everything Ertide had learned. Arandon's revelation had been the last chip that shattered the sword. The angels had to be resisted. God's will could not be done.

"What do you think of the decision, Jertis?" Ertide asked as he was wheeled down the corridor. Faces of kings past stared down at him from a succession of paintings.

"Me, sire?"

"Don't turn stupid on me now, Jertis."

The servant smiled. Ertide didn't need to look at him to know that. "It was quite a shock."

"Do you think it was the right decision?"

"It's not my place to say, sire."

"You'll answer my question."

Jertis coughed politely. "Only time will tell, sire."

"Impressive hedging, Jertis.

"Thank you."

Ertide closed his eyes and leaned back into his chair. "I'll make sure you're looked after, Jertis. Once I'm gone, whoever you serve next, I'll make sure you're treated well. Your family... Do you have a family?"

Jertis nodded, smiling. "A wife, Lancet. Two daughters, Merry and Poppen."

"I feel like that's something I should have known."

"Why would you, sire? I serve you, not the other way around."

Something Ertide had once read drifted into his mind. He'd been studying military philosophy in the hope of becoming a better leader, but every so often the author had drifted off on a tangent. He'd written: *Do the people serve the king, or does the king serve the people? Consider the circle. Strong and flexible, but a single break in the line and the structure falls apart. Therefore it might be better to say: The people DO serve the king, so that the king MAY serve the people.*

They were passing the King's Shrine and Jertis slowed them to a stop. The door was ajar. Ertide immediately patted his hip to find the key still in his pocket.

"Did you lock the door this morning after prayers, Jertis?"

"I'm sure of it, sire." Jertis looked around nervously. There were no guards here.

"Help me up," Ertide said.

"Sire, we should..."

"Help me up, Jertis."

Ertide reached his feet with a few grunts and more effort from Jertis than himself. His cane tapped the floor and he leaned on it heavily as he shuffled towards the open door. He wasn't sure what to expect. Caran, taking out petty spite on his father by destroying his shrine? The Rider waiting to ambush a king who had disobeyed him? Perhaps even the God himself, stepped from the halls of Heaven to tell Ertide what a naughty boy he'd been.

He slowly pushed the door all the way open. The shrine was chilly, the window thrown open wide. Far to the north, Heaven's light shone down from the sky, clear in the dark night. Along with the blazing bronze of the Bone Moon, it silhouetted a figure sitting on the windowsill. A small man with dark wings. Moon had returned at last.

"You can go, Jertis," Ertide said from the doorway.

"But sire..."

"Go!"

Ertide shuffled into the shrine, his cane tapping on the stone with every step. He pushed the door closed behind him, heard the click of the latch. Moon didn't move, didn't respond. He sat on the sill, one leg dangling either side, his head tilted to stare out into the city. His dark hair hung limp across his face, but Ertide could see his friend's lips moving.

"Moon?"

Moon's head tilted his way, but he didn't see Ertide. The angel's eyes were dark as tar, his seer's vision had hold of him.

"The viper cannot help but bite, its nature is to betray. But the wolf comes comes comes to free me. The wolf should not exist, does not exist. Must correct. Seven. Seven Exemplars. Seven Kings. Seven sacrifices. The Saint knew. Knew and did nothing, does nothing. But the daughter will, she will fight. In her own way. Seven. Seven blades to break the world. Seven years to save him. The Last Hope of the Dying cannot know the truth. Undying. Unburnt. A new terror rises. His sacrifice will save us all, but doom the one I love. The wolf comes. The wolf should not exist. Cannot correct. Why does the wolf always come?"

Ertide shuffled forwards and leaned against the sill. He took Moon's hand in his hand and squeezed tight. The angel stared right through him.

"The future grows more certain by the day. The past becomes a blur. The wolf closes in. She does not exist, but she must. She will free me. She mustn't free me."

Ertide leaned forward and squeezed Moon's hand a little tighter. "Moon. Stop it. Come back to me. Let go of it and just come back."

"Ertide?" Moon asked. His eyes were still dark, his head darted about as if trying to find him. "Are you there?"

"I'm here, Moon. Come back."

"I can't find my way. I'm scared. Seven chances to change the past. Seven hands covered in blood. The wolf, Ertide. The wolf is coming for me."

He reached up and cupped his friend's cheek. "There is no wolf, Moon. The wolf does not exist. Come back to me."

"The wolf does not exist," Moon repeated. "Does not exist. I can stop the wolf from freeing me." His eyes cleared, the darkness draining away like water down a drain until the whites reflected the gold of the Bone Moon shining down on them both.

Moon's face crumpled and tears streamed down his cheeks. "Oh, Ertide." He launched across the sill and wrapped his arms around Ertide, burying his face in his chest and sobbing. "I was gone. So lost. I couldn't find my way back."

"It's alright." Ertide stroked Moon's hair with his one good arm. "You're back now, old friend. You're here now."

Moon sobbed, clutching at Ertide like a drowning man to his last gulp of air. He always struggled after the sight took him, but it had never been this bad before. He'd never seemed so distraught before. Eventually the angel stopped crying and pulled back, wiping the tears from his eyes.

"Ertide..."

"What is it, Moon?"

"You look awful."

Ertide chuckled. "I feel worse. You've been gone months again, old friend. I... I'm dying."

Moon wiped another hand across his eyes, and smiled mischievously. "No, you're not. I won't let you."

"You remember then?"

Moon nodded. He was coming back to himself now. "I know what we need to do, Ertide. But it has to be soon. We don't have much time."

"Am I that close to death?"

Moon opened his mouth, then closed it again. It was all the answer Ertide needed.

"Then I suppose we should get on with it."

Moon leaned back against the frame of the window, turned his head to stare out across the city. Heaven's light blazed in the far distance.

"Before we go any further, you need to know how this ends." The angel sighed. "Nothing we have done so far cannot be forgotten, but if we go ahead, if we kill an angel for their blood, God will find out. Eventually. It cannot be hidden forever. You need to know, he is not merciful, and his wroth will be terrible. Unless you strike first."

"Strike first?"

"There is only one way this ends, Ertide. We will hide it from him for as long as possible, but before he finds out, you must gather humanity and forge them into a weapon. The only way this ends is with you taking the war to Heaven."

Ertide shifted. His entire body ached, the icy claws clutched at his heart. He considered his legacy, what he wanted to be remembered for. A war against Heaven? Against God, with his entire empire on the line.

Such a legacy I will leave.

"We cannot fight against Heaven unless the angels have a weakness."

"They do. We do. I can tell it to you, if you want. But this is it, old friend. Your last chance to back away. I have seen it so many times in so many ways. If I tell you this, you will have no choice but to go to war. Not now. Not today. But soon. A war that will consume your empire."

Ertide looked back into the shrine. His father's book sat on the wooden pew. His father's one act of rebellion against Heaven, to write down all he knew about the lies, and pass it on to his son. And Ertide had done nothing with it.

"Why are you doing this, Moon?" Ertide asked.

"To save you."

Ertide waved the vapid answer away with his hand. "Why are you doing this? Why condemn one of your siblings to death? Maybe more than one. Why would you betray God?"

Moon met his gaze and shrugged. "I would do anything to save the one I love. And only I can see the way to do it." He shook his head and stared up at the Bone Moon crawling across the sky.

"You are my anchor, Ertide. Without you, I am adrift. This curse of mine, this sight, it steals me, pulls me where it will like a capricious current. And when finally I surface, I am never where I was. The world changes around me and so much of what I saw in the current has become past already. So much of the future I see is made impossible. Why should I have this cursed sight if I cannot change things to make the world better?

"I have never met anyone else who can pull me out of the current, Ertide. Only you. My anchor, keeping me tethered to the world. I cannot lose you because I know that in that loss, I would lose myself as well. So I will do everything I can to save you. Because I love you. And I love me. I cannot lose you and I will not lose myself." He met Ertide's gaze and shrugged. "You are my anchor."

Ertide stared at his friend for a while. All the angels were so strong, so radiant. Even the angels of the Fourth Age, almost human in size, had an inevitability about them that made them seem invincible. But Moon was different. So fragile despite his strength.

"Your anchor," Ertide said. He grinned. "Bit of a tortured metaphor, don't you think?"

Moon wiped his eyes. "Would you like a worse one?" He raised a dramatic hand towards the sky. "You are the moons to my sun. I streak across the sky, dragging you behind me, and you but stop me from flying away."

Ertide snorted. "That was definitely worse."

Moon winked at him. "Now, while we're sharing. Why are you willing to do this, old friend? You dragged my reason from me, but what of yours? Why are you, the great King Ertide Hostain, willing to defy his own God?"

Ertide shrugged. "To save you? If I am your anchor, then I must live. It's only fair."

"Hmm. No! That's my reason. Get your own."

"I'm dying. I don't want to die, Moon."

"Oh, how very selfish. You don't want to die, so you're willing to take your entire empire to war. An unwinnable war. Truly, how great a king you are."

"Careful, Moon. You go too far."

"Noooo. No. I mean, all men fear death, I suppose. Why should you, great king, be any different? You're dying. That cannot be allowed. Other men might die, but not you. Not Ertide Hostain. He must not be allowed to die, even if it is God's will."

"God's will?" Ertide growled. "God's bloody will. Is it his will I should die, Moon? Is it? Like every other thing in my life, good or ill, is it really all by his shitting will? Damnit, Moon, I feel like I have no control. I *have* no control. I never did. I am a king without command of his kingdom. I am a man with no say over my own bloody life.

"I am told when to wake, to eat, when and how to pray. The decisions I make for my empire are not my decisions at all, but those allowed me by you angels and only then when I make the choices agreed for me. As is God's will.

"My wife... my bloody wife was chosen for me. She came to my bed every night to milk me in the hopes I would sire one more child. A child I'm so old I will never even meet. I am put out to stud like a bull. As is God's will."

"Yes, that does sound terrible."

"Do not belittle my pain, Moon. Do not! I have not had control over my own life since..." Ertide shook his head. "Since before I was even king. As is God's will. As is God's will. I don't give a damn about God's will. It's all a lie anyway. A fiction designed to control us, to pacify us."

Pain lanced through Ertide's chest and he clutched at his heart. The icy claws dug their talons deeper.

"If I do not act to change it now, if I don't take this chance you have presented me, my heir will suffer the same fate. They will have no control, and everyone who comes after them will have no control. Puppets designed to give the illusion of choice.

"So that is *my* reason, Moon. Because this is my chance, my one chance, to wrestle back control of my empire before God's will becomes the only will."

Moon pulled his knees up to his chest, hugged them. "Wrestle back control? You think you ever had it?"

Ertide shrugged. "I know the truth, Moon."

"Do you?"

"We were demons once. We had control then."

A slow smile crept across Moon's face. "Now that is interesting." He leaned forwards. "Time to learn the secret, Ertide. Time to learn how to kill an angel."

CHAPTER 19

Arandon pushed Ertide along in his chair. They couldn't risk even Jertis knowing about their secret meeting. There would be only eight of them, and even that many was dangerous until their loyalties were secure.

Bind them with three chains. Fear. Greed. Pride.

Moon sauntered along beside them, his wings draped over his shoulders in such a way they looked like a feathered cloak. He wore a hood also, and the disguise was surprisingly effective. Even Ertide wouldn't have recognised him for an angel, had he not already known.

They were running out of time. Not just for Ertide's ebbing life, but to pull all their pieces together. This meeting had to take place before the members went their separate ways. With Springtide days gone, some of them should already have returned to their homes. And for Ertide's plan to work, they needed precise timing. God's eyes would need to be elsewhere and Moon had claimed he could do that but only once. All he needed was to borrow one of the twins. He had chosen Emrik, but was adamant he could not be in on the plan. For now, Emrik remained oblivious, and therefore so too did Merian. The twins were ever terrible at hiding secrets from each other.

The next part of the plan was to be rid of the Heralds. Mathanial,

Orphus, and Eleseth all needed to be out of the city. Arandon had come up with the solution to that. The Rider's first ship would soon be launched, and so they would make a ceremony of it. A grand celebration. Of course, they needed some legitimacy to it. Ertide couldn't travel to Vale where the ships were being built, he was too ill. Arandon's position as heir was still too new. So they would send Caran with the angels. And to secure his cooperation, Arandon had ordered the name for the ship to be changed. *Caran's Ambition*. It would be launched in two weeks.

Almost everything was in place except for this. They needed allies. They needed family. They needed to bind them.

"Are you sure about this, Grandfather?" Arandon asked as they stopped before the door. Two soldiers stood outside, both wearing the black and a single gold stripe of the First Legion, and both wearing the crimson armbands of Rikkan's chosen.

"Bit late to turn back now if he isn't," Moon said flippantly.

"It's not too late," Arandon said. "Nothing has yet been done that cannot be undone."

"Like naming you heir?" Moon asked, grinning. "Quick, call him back and put Caran on the throne. Tell me, young heir, how long do you think you would survive? How long before your dear uncle found a way to... remove you?"

"He wouldn't," Arandon said.

Moon simpered. "You're right, of course. How could I be so foolish?"

"Enough," Ertide snapped. "Both of you. Arandon, you're not king yet. Not while I still breathe. Moon, stop being an arse."

The soldiers pushed open the door and Moon scampered through. Arandon pushed Ertide's chair into a round chamber wide enough to walk a bull around. It had no windows, and only the one door which closed behind them. It was as secure as they could make it, lit only by flickering candle light. A circular table sat in the centre, seven chairs arrayed around it. On the table's surface was a fresco of the Saint and her six Knights Exemplar. A fitting place to hatch a plot against Heaven.

"Ha!" Renshin barked. "One last bit of drama from you, brother? I love it!" He was lounging in one of the chairs, its feet rocked back so he had his military boots, polished to a shine, resting on the table. He also had a flagon of wine in hand.

Rikkan leaned against the far wall, his arms crossed over his chest, his dark eyes piercing. He already knew most of what was happening. He was already bound to the cause.

Mertred sat straight-backed, her hand on a wine goblet. She spun the goblet around and around slowly. "These clandestine meetings do not suit me, father."

"Ha!" Renshin said. "Cheer up, niece. No need to be so dour. Your father used to love pulling shit like this. Made life exciting. Remember that time you had us sneak into the brothel and spy on old uncle Ulis being whipped and walked around on a leash like a dog? Damned exciting stuff."

"Excitement is overrated, uncle." This was from Kurtis Hostain. The fraying rope of a man stood behind his chair, hands clutching the back like a vulture on a perch. He was the son of Ertide's sister, Iosin and the magistrate of Bresh over in the Ashlands. He was perhaps the least certain Ertide was of trusting, but he had a reputation as a pragmatic man. More importantly, he had the position they needed.

"Well, it's easy to see who the odd one out here is," the final member of their conspiracy said as she paced back and forth in front of Rikkan, as if taunting him. Jacklin Hostain was plump as a goose ready for plucking. She looked soft, but it was all for show. Jacklin was Renshin's granddaughter and had been a prodigy in the boxing rings in her younger years. "I'm the only one here not suckling on the teat of power."

Ertide smiled and Renshin roared in laughter. A long time ago, Jacklin had been in the running for a prime position as mayor of Gurrund. She didn't want it. So when Eleseth had offered her the position, Jacklin told the angel to *piss off*, and then spat on her shoes. She had since been all but banished and now ran a tavern in the eastern city of Everheim. Renshin was quite proud of the fact that the tavern was really just a front for an underground gambling network. Jacklin had no love for the angels, and contacts all over the empire. She was a perfect choice.

It made seven of them, eight if Ertide included Moon. The angel picked his way carefully around the table and chose the chair that was obviously meant for Rikkan. He sat down without ceremony, then leaned back over the chair and winked at the prince. Rikkan ignored him.

"What's this all about then, brother?" Renshin asked. "You got us all here. Mind telling us why?"

Arandon helped Ertide out of his wheeled chair and he shuffled forward, walking around the table, his cane tapping.

Bind them with greed.

"Are you content, Renshin? With the life you have been given? With the years you have left? What about you, Jacklin? Kurtis? Are you happy with your paltry handful of years while angels live forever? Immortal. Eternal." He paced around as he walked, slowly shuffling step after step.

"I am the oldest one here. My life is almost at an end. And let me tell you. It. Was. Not. Enough. So much left undone, unsaid, unexperienced. Enemies left unkilled and lovers left unbedded. And yet I am supposed to be content with what I have been given while angels live on despite having done nothing to earn it. I am not content. I want more. I want to live. Do you?"

He walked in front of Rikkan and his eldest son gave him a slight nod.

"Do you all want more? Longer lives. Healthy lives. Are you happy and content with your lot? The way your knees ache, your breath tightens, the pounding head from too much ale? Or do you want the same immortality an angel enjoys?"

Renshin kept his gaze on Ertide, narrowed and calculating. He liked to play the loud, stupid soldier, but he'd always been keener of mind than he let on. Kurtis' face was stone, unreadable and unyielding. But Jacklin, she was already invested by the way she leaned in, the tug of a smile on her lips. She glanced at Moon. Moon gave her a foolish little wave with his fingers.

"How?" This came from Kurtis. Perhaps more interested than he was letting on. A calm surface over churning rapids.

Bind them with fear.

"This is where I warn you," Ertide said. "What I'm going to tell you next will get you killed if the angels ever find out."

Renshin coughed loudly. "Brother, I don't know if you've noticed, but there is an angel in the room."

"Oh don't worry about me," Moon said. He leaned back in his chair and placed his sandals on the table, imitating Renshin's posture. "I'm one of the *good* ones. The only good one, really."

"This is your chance to leave," Ertide continued. "Now. If you stay, you leverage your lives, and the lives of everyone you love. This is God's best kept secret and he will destroy anyone he suspects of knowing." He stopped behind Arandon and turned to face them all. "I picked you all because I think you are brave, but if any of you is a coward, now is the time to go."

He waited, hoping none would leave. Hoping Rikkan wouldn't have to kill any of them.

No one moved.

Ertide smiled at them all. "Angel blood is the key. If we drink it, we steal their immortality. If we eat their flesh, we steal their strength."

This time Kurtis turned his head slowly to look at Moon.

"Not me!" Moon said quickly. "Still one of the good ones. Also, I'd taste horrible. Too much vinegar in the diet."

A nasty smile spread across Kurtis' face. "I like pickles."

Moon took his feet from the table and scooted his chair away, the legs scraping loudly across the floor. "Well, regardless, if you kill me, God will know." He stuck a pink tongue out at Kurtis.

"Pointless," Mertred said, speaking for the first time. "Father, I have fought beside angels. I've seen them take hits that would skewer a man, armour be damned. They rise with not even a scratch on them. Angels are impervious."

"She's right," Renshin chimed in. "They're immortal, brother. Can't be killed."

Bind them with pride.

"You forget your history, brother," Ertide said. He desperately wanted to sit down, his legs trembling from the effort, but he needed to stand. He needed to show strength. "Angels can die. In the First Age, many angels died."

Renshin snorted. "To the demons, yes."

The trap sprung. "There were no demons. They were but the lie told to capture our hearts. There was only ever us, humans. And them, angels."

Renshin took his feet from the table and leaned forwards. Mertred glanced over her shoulder at Rikkan, standing still and coiled like a cat ready to pounce. Kurtis smiled again. Jacklin was the one to push to her feet, hands balled into fists on the table. She stared at Moon.

"Is it true?"

"Is what true?" Moon asked. "Be more specific."

"There were no demons. Or we were, are the demons?"

Moon grinned a wide, knowing smile.

"Damn." Jacklin fell back into her chair. "Damn damn damn."

"Demons were the lie sold to justify the angels' pacification of humanity," Ertide continued. "And ever since, we have been thralls to a lying God. We pray to our master, the one holding the leashes around our necks. We obey the angels, the ones who slaughtered us to bring us to heel. But once we were strong. We fought back. We killed our enemies." He swept his gaze around them all. "We can be strong again."

"How?" Mertred asked, her hands steepled before her. "How do we kill them, father?"

Moon's hand shot into the air like a child begging the attention of his tutor. Even now, everything was a joke to him. "Oh, I know. I know! We angels have a weakness, a flaw. You see, it's our immortality shields that make us impervious to your weapons. But..." He paused and leaned forward dramatically. "They can be shattered."

"How?" Rikkan asked.

Moon stared at him. "By killing humans. The more lives we angels take, the weaker our connection to God becomes. If we take too many lives, that connection breaks. Our immortality shields shatter. Then we can die as easily as you. Poke us with a spear, slash us with a sword, burn us with fire. You know, all the classics."

"How many?" Mertred asked darkly. "How many lives do we have to sacrifice to break an angel?"

Moon shrugged. "I don't know. One of my siblings from the First Age?" He whistled. "Many. They were born to kill. Their connection to God is strong. But an angel from the Fourth Age? Hmm, not so many."

"I have a plan," Ertide said, finally taking his seat. "Two weeks from now, we will all be immortal. Assuming you are all invested."

"I'm in," Rikkan said quickly. He hadn't moved from his spot against the far wall, but a smile tugged at his lips. He was thinking of fighting an angel on even terms. A fight he could finally win.

"As am I," Arandon said, his first and only words. He looked at his father for approval, but Rikkan looked away.

"Well, I feel a little ensnared, to be honest, brother," Renshin said. "But sure, why not? I feel the pull of age dragging me to the grave, and I do not like it. Give me this immortality."

Kurtis' eyes narrowed. He glanced at Rikkan behind him, then back to Ertide. "Why us?" He nodded at Jacklin. "I don't know you, uncle. This is only the second time we've met and the first time we've spoken. So why me?"

Ertide smiled at his nephew. "Because I need you. I need your position. This is only the start of things. I am playing the long game and I am playing to win. And to be entirely honest, I need people I can trust in the east."

"And you can trust me?"

"Agree to this and I can. We will be bound in more ways than you know."

Kurtis' gaze shifted around the room. "And if I don't agree?"

Ertide said nothing. No words were needed.

"Hmm. I thought so. I appreciate your honesty, my king. I'm in."

Ertide looked to Jacklin. The woman grinned.

"Immortality can be taken, given. It is a new product, one without value. That means we can determine its value." She nodded to herself. "The price will be very high. I'm in."

That left only Mertred. She sat with her hands steepled, her gaze boring into the wooden table and its fresco of the Saint, their ancient ancestor.

"Dien was supposed to be the best of us," Mertred said. "She who rose up when no one else would. Who allied with the angels, united humanity, freed us from our shackles. Was it all a lie then? The Saint did not free us, she chained us."

Mertred slowly turned her head until she was staring at Moon, her gaze was hostile. "You took away our dignity, angel. You named us monsters, demons." Her eyes flicked to Ertide. "We will show them how monstrous we can be."

CHAPTER 20

The day approached so rapidly, Ertide didn't feel ready. Everything was falling into place, all his plans and preparations, and yet there was always so much more to do. So much more to consider.

Caran had recently departed for Vael, Orphus and Mathanial going with him. They would be gone for days, weeks maybe, celebrating the launch of *Caran's Ambition*, the first step in the Rider's grand expedition. Eleseth, however, had chosen to stay behind. They needed to find a way to get her out of the palace. There could be no other angels around when they sprung their trap, and Moon had been adamant, they were not prepared to tangle with Eleseth. The Herald of the Second Age was fire incarnate when she got worked up.

There was still the issue of distracting God as well. Moon had claimed he could do it, that he would only need Emrik, but Moon had vanished again and was yet to return. The icy talons clawed at Ertide's heart.

They cleared the west wing of the palace of everyone but soldiers of the First Legion, those Rikkan had claimed as his own. The official excuse was for renovations of the Grand Samir courtyard. It provided the perfect excuse.

The day before the plot, Ertide was dozing in his study when a hard knock sounded at the door. He almost fell out of his chair. Jertis opened the door and Eleseth stooped under the doorframe as she stepped in. It never ceased to amaze Ertide how radiant the Herald of the Second Age was. Even now, knowing everything he did, and so close to death as he was, he felt his blood stir at the sight of her. Such beauty. Eleseth truly was born to inspire worship.

"How are you feeling today, Ertide?" Eleseth asked as she knelt by his side.

"Old," Ertide said with a laugh that quickly turned into a cough.

Without asking, Eleseth reached out and laid a hand against his chest. She glowed with the light of a forest fire, and her warmth penetrated Ertide, easing the icy claws around his heart. He breathed deeper than he had for weeks.

"I know it's not much," Eleseth said as her glow faded. The room seemed so much darker without her radiant glow. "But all I can do is ease your pain."

He patted her giant hand gently and smiled at her. "It is enough," he lied.

"I have a request, Ertide," the angel said as she stood. "I need to borrow your grandson. Emrik."

Moon's part of the plan in action. "Borrow him?"

Eleseth's smile brightened the room again. "My father wishes to speak to him."

Ertide widened his eyes, hoping his surprise didn't look too forced. If his poor acting gave the ruse away now, it would all be over. "Your father... God wants to speak to Emrik?"

Eleseth chuckled and laughed. "It is a great honour. The greatest of honours. I'm to send Emrik north, to Heaven's Gate."

Ertide leaned forwards in his chair, conspiratorially. "Not really a request, is it?" He smiled.

Eleseth shook her head.

"I will allow it," Ertide said with a wide grin. "On one condition. We break the news to him together. I want to see the shock on his face."

They sent for Emrik, while Eleseth led Ertide up through the palace to the Sky Garden. It was a flat rooftop on the eastern wing of the palace. Ornate planters lined the garden, each one filled with flowers and herbs, colours and scents Ertide could barely name. The garden was open to the sky and many angels used it to land when visiting the palace. So, too, it seemed, did pegasi. One of the winged horses was waiting there, its wings furled at its side, white fur gleaming in the afternoon light. It looked up at them when they reached the rooftop, then snorted and bent its head to one of the planters and ripped up a blue flower by the stem, chewing it lazily.

Emrik was alone when he arrived. His hair was tousled from sleep, and he had rings under his eyes. His dark blue jacket was ruffled as if he had slept in it.

"What's this about, Grandfather?" Emrik asked around a yawn as he climbed the last steps and staggered out from the stairwell into the light. "I was sleeping away a very pleasant evening spent with…" He stopped when he saw Eleseth standing beside Ertide.

"Oh, hello." Emrik grinned and straightened down his jacket and ran a hand through his hair.

Ertide rolled his eyes. All well knew of Emrik's foolish infatuation with the Light Bringer.

Eleseth let Ertide break the *good* news. He secretly enjoyed watching his grandson's face turn from smug to fear.

"Why me?" Emrik asked. "What have I done?"

Eleseth chuckled. "You haven't done anything. It's an honour."

"Right." Emrik paced, glanced at the pegasus, then back to Eleseth. "I could do with a drink, Jertis. Wine."

Jertis looked to Ertide. Ertide shook his head.

"Damnit!" Emrik said. He was scared. "Nobody is honoured without having done something, and I make a point of doing nothing. So what have I done?"

"Just go, Emrik," Ertide said. "It'll be an experience. One nobody else can claim. The first of our family to meet God in… many generations."

Eleseth gestured towards the pegasus. "Your ride awaits."

"What?" Emrik shook his head. "You want me to ride one of those beasts? No! Merian would knock my teeth out."

"You're scared," Ertide said.

"Too right, I am, Grandfather. It's a bloody horse with wings."

Ertide sensed an opportunity. "Eleseth, will you go with him? Hold my poor grandson's hand."

Eventually they cajoled Emrik onto the pegasus. Eleseth claimed the flight would take a day to Heaven's Gate, and another back again after Emrik had met God. Ertide hoped his grandson would be alright. He had to trust that Moon would not sacrifice him for their heresy, and there could be no doubt that this was Moon's doing. Yet still the Apostle did not return. Regardless, everything was now in place. Ertide had no choice but to go ahead with the plan and hope for the best.

CHAPTER 21

Ertide couldn't sleep. He was exhausted, but he spent the entire night tossing and turning, expecting to hear shouts of alarm and the fluttering of angelic wings at any moment. Expecting to be discovered. When Jertis came to wake him, he was already sitting in his bed, a sticky sheen of sweat covering his skin.

The day had arrived. All their planning led to this.

He picked at his breakfast: a crumb of bread here, a grape there. It was all he could manage. After that he went to the King's Shrine to *pray*, hoping he would find Moon waiting for him there. The angel was absent.

A sick dread wormed into Ertide's guts. Perhaps it had all been a ruse from the beginning. Moon acting on God's orders. A way to expose and do away with the entire family, pull out the weed by its roots. He cursed himself for a fool. Moon was his oldest friend. He would trust the angel. He had to.

After morning prayers, he had Jertis wheel him to his study. Ertide spent a few moments rooting about his desk until he found the plans for the Grand Samir courtyard. The architects were still awaiting his choice before work could start.

Jertis almost argued when Ertide ordered him to run off to Arkenhold University and fetch Oronesus, but the man knew better. Ertide said he would meet the Bookkeeper in the courtyard, where they would go over the plans and decide together.

Once Jertis was gone, Rikkan strode into the study. He was dressed for battle, leather armour sewn with metal plates, his spear in a harness across his back. Two of his crimson armband soldiers walked with him.

"Are they ready?" Ertide asked quietly as Rikkan wheeled him towards the courtyard.

"They are," Rikkan didn't need to ask to know Ertide meant the soldiers.

"Will they fight?"

A moment's silence. "They will."

One question remained unspoken. *Will they die?* They would. Ertide told himself soldiers always died in battle. It was no different to his assault on Fort Deishel so many years ago. He had sent his men to assault the gates, knowing they would fail and some would die. A distraction.

This is no different. It's no different.

The Grand Samir courtyard was a large open space built in a square. The ground itself was bare earth, muddy and strewn with weeds and tufts of grass. It had been dug out months ago, waiting for Ertide to make his decision on the design. A few old tools, a spade, a wheelbarrow, lay around, forgotten. High pillars surrounded the courtyard on all sides, each one carved from stone. A dozen doors led off from all corners into the palace. Above, tall windows looked down on the space, so those in the nearby rooms could watch the courtyard. Those rooms had been empty for years. Not anymore. Now they were filled with soldiers, all of them armed with bows. More soldiers hid nearby on the ground floor, waiting for the signal. And on the rooftops as well, twenty of Rikkan's soldiers hid bellies to the stone, out of sight.

"Nervous, son?" Ertide asked as they waited.

"No."

He couldn't tell if Rikkan was joking or not. Probably not. His eldest had never had a sense of humour. Even as a child he had always been so serious. Giliana had despaired over trying to make her son laugh.

Arandon was next to arrive. His nerves showed in the way he walked, the way he kept looking around as if expecting the angel to jump out from behind a pillar.

"The others are here, waiting. Hiding." Arandon licked his lips. "I…"

"Compose yourself," Rikkan snarled.

Arandon quieted and clasped his trembling hands together, chastised by his father despite being heir to the crown. He would need to break that habit.

They waited.

Jertis was the first through the doorway on the southern side of the courtyard, Oronesus just a few steps behind him. She was wearing a brown robe just a shade lighter than her skin, and her book satchel hung heavy at her hip. Her hawk's wings ruffled as she glanced about the courtyard and saw Rikkan and Arandon with Ertide.

"Ertide?" Oronesus asked. "I thought we were to discuss the plans for the courtyard?"

"Do we wait?" Rikkan asked quietly.

She was twenty steps away, crossing the earth towards them. She couldn't be allowed to get close, not until her shield was broken.

In battle, in war, in negotiation, in diplomacy, and in love, there was no greater advantage than that of surprise.

"Do it!" Ertide said.

Rikkan raised his fingers to his mouth and whistled sharp and loud.

The Bookkeeper slowed to a stop, glancing about as the tramp of boots rang out across stone. Soldiers poured into the courtyard from every doorway, swords drawn, spears held at the ready. Others stepped up to windows, bows ready with arrows knocked. Above, a dozen soldiers ran across the rooftops, dragging a heavy chain-linked net across to stop the angel from escaping via the sky.

Oronesus stared about at the soldiers, looked up as the chain links settled into position and even more soldiers with bows crowded the rooftop. The Bookkeeper did not panic or rage. She appeared icily calm.

"What is the meaning of this, Ertide?"

The arrogance of her. Even now she cannot conceive of treachery.

"Jertis," Ertide called out from his chair. "Get out of the way."

Jertis' eyes were wide with shock, but he slowly walked away from the angel. As he neared the edge of the courtyard, one of Rikkan's soldiers grabbed him and pulled him away. Oronesus was left alone in the centre of the bare earth.

"Explain yourself, Ertide," Oronesus said, her voice hard now.

Beside Ertide, Arandon wrung his hands together, nervous. Renshin, Mertred, Jacklin, and Kurtis moved up to join them, the seven conspirators standing together.

Rikkan glanced down at Ertide. "Do we let her talk, father?"

Ertide shook his head. "She has nothing to say I wish to hear. Get on with it."

Rikkan took a single step forward and drew his spear from over his back. He pointed it at the Bookkeeper. She had just one moment to frown in confusion, before the first wave of Rikkan's soldiers charged into the courtyard.

The first soldier to reach the angel was a man with a scruffy beard and a spear. He slid to a stop and thrust. The spear tip smashed into Oronesus' sternum. The angel grunted, winced in pain, but there was no blood, no wound. She turned a furious gaze on the man, snapped the spear haft in two and backhanded the soldier so hard he spun away through the air and didn't get up.

The first wave was ten soldiers strong. They slashed with swords, stabbed with spears, bludgeoned with maces. Oronesus waded through the blows, howling in pain each time they struck flesh, but still she did not wound. She reached out through the thicket of spears, grabbed a soldier by the helm and crushed it with one hand, he dropped dead, blood seeping out the wound. She snapped another soldier's neck as easily a child would a twig. A sword got caught in her robes, she grabbed it, crushed the soldier's hand against the hilt, then buried the blade in her face. All the while, other soldiers stabbed at her. She didn't try to defend herself, only weathered the storm and barrelled through it, slaughtering anyone she could reach.

"It's interesting, is it not," Ertide said as he watched. "That she cannot be wounded, but she can feel pain."

One of the soldiers scored a lucky hit on her knee, and Oronesus screamed and collapsed. The remaining four soldiers of the first wave closed in, hacking and stabbing brutally. Oronesus shielded her face with her hands as sharp steel flashed and bounced off her skin as surely as it would stone.

"ENOUGH!" The angel roared back to her feet, thrusting out her wings and throwing the soldiers back. She caught one of the men as he fell, slammed him to the ground by his breastplate, then stamped so hard on his head his skull burst.

Oronesus turned to Ertide, her face a picture of fury. "I do not know what is happening here, but you will burn for this, Ertide."

Rikkan raised his hand and lowered it sharply. The twang of a hundred bowstrings filled the air and the angel screamed in pain as a hundred arrows found their mark, driving her back to her knees. Her robes were already tattered, barely rags from the number of strikes she had suffered, and stained with the blood of so many humans, yet none of it hers. Her satchel had come loose, the strap severed, her precious books strewn across the muddy ground.

Slowly, the angel staggered back to her feet. She pulled an arrow from where it had tangled in her robes and flicked her hand to the side. The shaft flew as if shot from a bow and a soldier screamed and fell from one of the windows. Again Oronesus locked her angry gaze on Ertide. She took a thunderous step towards him.

"Second wave!" Rikkan shouted.

A moment's hesitation. The soldiers had seen what the angel could do now. They had seen she was impervious to sword and spear and arrow. They were scared.

Mertred drew her sword and roared. Her battle cry was picked up by the soldiers and reverberated around the courtyard. She charged and soldiers charged with her, waves be damned.

Mertred reached the angel first, stabbing. Oronesus flowed around the sword strike so easily. She turned, battered Mertred with a wing and sent her tumbling away. Then the soldiers hit her.

Men and women died quickly now. Oronesus was no longer holding back. She leapt ten feet into the air, landed on a man and crushed him into the earth. She plucked a sword from the hand of a woman and tossed it casually away with such strength it skewered another soldier. The angel tore arms from their sockets, ripped out throats, crushed skulls. It was all so easy to her. A child kicking over sandcastles. The blows she weathered hurt her still, but it was just pain. No sword could pierce her, no blow could break bones, no press of bodies could hold her down.

Ertide felt those icy claws tightening around his heart again as fear crept in. He'd battled beside angels before, seen them fight. They were deadly on the battlefield, yes, but not like this. He realised then, he had never seen an angel fight for their life before. It was terrifying.

She is an angel of the Fourth Age. Moon said they were the weakest of God's children.

Mertred had reached the edge of the courtyard now, pulled her self back to her feet using a pillar. She was clutching at her ribs. Other soldiers were crawling away from the battle, too, those too wounded to fight on.

Oronesus looked like she was straining, grimacing as she picked up a soldier by his throat, snapped his neck and tossed his body into another. She waded forwards another step.

"ERTIDE!" the angel screamed. A woman barrelled into her, clutched at her waist, stabbed a dagger into her side again and again. Oronesus grabbed her by her breastplate and wrenched her upwards, throwing the woman twenty feet into the air, only to crash back to the ground behind her.

"My soldiers are dying, father," Rikkan said through a clenched jaw. "How many more?"

Ertide grimaced but didn't look away from the fight. "As many as it takes."

"Sire, what is this?" Jertis asked.

"Quiet!" Ertide snapped.

The courtyard was growing brighter now, he was sure of it. A bright white light that chased away all shadows. Oronesus screamed. The angel was on her knees, a hand clutching her chest, but she was not wounded. Soldiers stabbed at her. A bear of a man dashed in, wrapped his gauntleted hands around her throat, squeezed. Oronesus' eyes goggled and she reached up, grabbed the bear's throat and tore it out. The light grew blinding, so bright Ertide had to shield his eyes.

"Finally," he breathed. "Her shield breaks."

The light was so bright, Ertide squeezed his eyes shut and still he could see it. Oronesus screamed. Soldiers screamed. Then they didn't.

Ertide heard the rustle of paper fluttering, of pages turning, of scrolls rolling and rasping against themselves.

It was over. The light faded slowly and Ertide blinked away bright spots to look upon a field of carnage.

CHAPTER 22

Oronesus knelt in the middle of the courtyard, surrounded by soldiers clawing at their eyes. Only they weren't soldiers anymore. An errant breeze gusted into the space and one of the soldiers unrolled into a thousand sheets of paper and fluttered away to fall across the courtyard. Dozens of soldiers, all those who had been close to the angel when her shield broke, were now nothing but statues made of paper. On the ground, seared into the earth itself was a symbol of an open book, an archway scrawled across the pages. The Bookkeeper's angelic emblem.

The angel stood on unsteady legs. Her wings brushed against one of the paper statues and it fell, pages peeling apart. "What have you done?" she said.

"My turn?" Rikkan asked.

Ertide nodded. With her immortality shield broken, the Bookkeeper was weakened, vulnerable. This was what had bound Rikkan so easily to the cause, the chance to fight an angel on equal footing. The chance to test himself against an opponent who could truly challenge him.

"Finally," Rikkan strode forwards into the courtyard. "I am unleashed!" His walk turned into a sprint.

Oronesus leapt into the air with a beat of her wings that sent more paper statues fluttering. She hit the chain links above, ripped at them, trying to escape.

A crossbow bolt flew from the ground floor of the courtyard and slammed into her left wing, piercing the bone with a spray of blood. The angel screamed in agony. There was a rope attached to the bolt and two soldiers tugged on it, bringing the angel crashing back to the ground in a heap.

Rikkan closed on the angel and swept out with his spear, slicing through the rope. As Oronesus tried to rise, Rikkan spun about and brought his spear down. The bladed tip struck bone and sliced through the angel's wounded wing, severing it. Oronesus howled, staggered back, her left wing lying lifeless on the ground, red blood seeping into the earth.

"Beast!" the angel screamed at Rikkan.

Rikkan held back, waiting for the Bookkeeper to gather herself. "No one else is to get involved," he said loudly. "This fight is mine."

Oronesus laughed savagely, winced, staggered back, laughed again. "Such arrogance to think you can best me alone."

Rikkan waited, still and straight as his spear. "You confuse honour with arrogance, angel. Prepare yourself."

Oronesus took a steadying breath and stood up straight. She was taller than Rikkan, but not by much. Slimmer, but she radiated a strength no human could match. Her robes were tattered and bloody, whereas Rikkan was pristine in his armour, yet the angel, even wounded, looked a titan.

The paper strewn about the courtyard started to flutter as if caught by a breeze, rising and twirling in the air. Oronesus glanced toward Ertide.

"You lose a son, here, Ertide," she smiled savagely at him. "It is only the beginning of what we will take from you."

Paper twisted, folded into feathers, wrapped into bones, welded itself to the stump of the angel's left wing. In moments she was whole again, one wing of flesh and feather and bone, and the other formed of paper. Oronesus gave it an experimental beat and smiled at the result.

"You may want a weapon, angel," Rikkan said.

The Bookkeeper laughed condescendingly. "Foolish human. We are surrounded by my weapons."

Rikkan launched forward, driving his spear for her chest. The angel raised a slender hand and sheets of paper whipped from the ground, wrapping around each other, and formed into a circular shield of paper. Rikkan's spear hit the shield, thudded to a stop. He leapt back, pulling his spear free. Oronesus did not follow. Her shield fell apart, individual sheets of paper fluttering to the ground.

"You really have no idea what we are capable of, human," the angel said in an icy voice.

One of the remaining paper statues lurched to life, swinging a paper sword at Rikkan. He slipped away, swept his spear around and through the statue. The papers scattered, losing shape, falling lifeless to the earth. The last two statues staggered for him. Rikkan batted a paper spear away, then thrust his own through the statue's head and ripped it sideways, decapitating the statue. The paper fell apart. The last statue had no weapon, ran at him. Rikkan ducked, slid backwards, lashed out with his spear so the statue tripped over the haft and hit the ground. Again the papers scattered, lost their shape. Still Oronesus didn't move. She stood, feather and paper wings outstretched as if ready for flight, her eyes fixed on her prey.

The Bookkeeper flicked her fingers and sheets of scattered paper coiled together, forming into a spike and driving at Rikkan. He danced away only for another spike to strike at him from the other side. It grazed his thigh, cutting through his leathers like a knife through butter. Rikkan was surrounded by sheets of fallen paper, they littered the ground between him and the angel.

"Damn him and his honour," Renshin said. "We should rush her."

"Fire," Ertide said. "Fetch fire. Burn away her paper."

"No!" Rikkan shouted. "I do this alone, father."

Oronesus leapt into the air again, her wings beating lazily to keep her floating ten feet off the ground. She swept her hands upwards and sheets of paper all across the courtyard shot skywards, slicing through metal chains. One of the soldiers screamed, cut short into a bloody gurgle, toppled from the rooftop. Chain links fell all around, jingling to the ground. The courtyard was open once more and there was nothing to stop the angel from escaping.

"Shoot her!" Ertide roared, leaning forward in his chair.

Bowstrings thrummed and arrows filled the air. Oronesus ducked, darted, swept around, dodging shafts. A few struck home, stealing feathers or sheets of paper from her wings, but none pierced the angel.

Oronesus floated in the air, her wings beating. She pointed a single finger. "We'll be coming for you, Ertide. All of you."

Rikkan's spear slammed into the angel, skewering her through her guts. She screamed, her wings desperately beating to keep her aloft. Rikkan, his spear already thrown, snatched a sword from the ground and launched into a sprint. Oronesus wept her hands forward and every loose sheet of paper in the courtyard twisted and spun, folding into a hundred spikes and thrusting at Rikkan. He dodged, twirled, jumped off one thrusting spike onto another and leapt at the angel. They collided mid air and both man and angel screamed in pain.

They hit the ground, rolling, Rikkan on top. His borrowed sword was in Oronesus' side, his spear snapped in half still lodged in her gut. The angel lay on her back, gasping, reached for Rikkan's head. He drew back, pulling his sword free and then drove it down into her chest. Oronesus spasmed and then relaxed limp and dead. Her paper wing and the spikes littering the courtyard lost their form and fell away, discarded sheets of paper once more.

Rikkan stood unsteadily over the body. He was hurt, wounds covered his legs and arms. Blood sheeted from a cut above his eye. His armour was a mess, covered in dust and blood. His hair was sweat coated and ragged. But he had won. The first human in two thousand years to kill an angel.

Ertide leaned forward in his chair and grinned. *It can be done!* The icy talons clutched at his heart and he coughed, felt blood in his mouth, warm on his lips.

Rikkan reached out to the side and clicked his fingers impatiently. One of his soldiers rushed forwards with a leather jack. Rikkan wrenched his borrowed sword from the angel's side and drained blood into the jack, then he turned and strode across the courtyard towards Ertide.

"Drink, father," Rikkan said, holding out the mug.

Ertide couldn't stop coughing. The talons were sharp, digging into his heart, tearing at his chest. He tried to reach for the jack, but couldn't lift his hand. Then Rikkan was kneeling at his side, holding the cup to his lips.

"Drink, father."

Someone gasped loudly. Ertide blocked it all out and gulped down the blood spilling past his lips.

CHAPTER 23

Pain lanced through Ertide as his chest was ripped apart, his bones shattered, his flesh torn asunder. He shook, trembled, convulsed in his chair, bit his tongue. His vision flared white. He heard voices everywhere calling his name. Hands held him to his chair. He was dying. Dying. His chest was so tight it must burst.

Then it was over. The pain drained away as water through a sieve, leaving only Ertide. He sweated, panted, slouched in his chair. The memory of agony was still so recent he could almost feel it all over again. He sucked in a breath. There was no rattle in his lungs, no cage around his heart. He could breathe. As if to taunt his recent weakness, he drew in air until he couldn't anymore then let it all out in a laughing burst.

"Father?" Rikkan's voice. No worry in the tone, his eldest son would never show concern.

"I'm..." Ertide panted, laughed again. "I'm alright. I'm... better than alright."

He opened his eyes to find Rikkan and Arandon watching him. Mertred waited nearby, clutching an arm across her chest as she watched. Renshin had hold of Ertide's shoulders, it had been his younger brother holding him down in the chair. Jacklin and Kurtis stood watching along with many of the soldiers.

Ertide grinned and flexed his arm, his bad arm, the one he hadn't been able to use for weeks now. It felt weak and weary, but he could move it again. He leaned forward in his chair and used Arandon as support as he pulled himself up. He stood there on his own two feet as he hadn't for so long. He didn't even need his cane. He was weak, yes, but from disuse rather than illness and fragility.

"I am cured," he said, grinning around at his chosen allies. "Cured of infirmity, of... of age. I am..." He looked down at his hands. They didn't seem any different, still wrinkled and spotted, gnarled from poor appetite and no work. But no more did they ache when he flexed his fingers. The chill of spring did not bite as hard. Even the twinge in his back, the shooting pains he had felt in his knees for decades. Gone.

"I am immortal," he said slowly. Then he turned as spryly as he had at twenty. "I am deathless."

Rikkan was the next to drink, gulping blood from the jack like it was the finest mead. Though in truth it tasted far sweeter than any wine or ale. He couldn't explain it, but Oronesus' blood had tasted like a warm hearth after a day in the snow and winter spices. Ertide wanted more.

Angel blood will make you immortal. Angel flesh will make you strong. That's what Moon said.

The jack was refilled from Oronesus' leaking body as soldiers crept closer to the corpse like starving wolves to a bear's kill. Arandon was next to drink, collapsing back against the pillar as the blood fixed his aches and pains. Then it was Renshin gulping from the mug, then Mertred, crying out as her ribs set about mending themselves. Finally Jacklin and Kurtis drank.

"We are bound together now," Ertide said to them. "We seven. Godless Kings, all of us. And I will see you all kings in your own right. I will need you all for what is to come. This is only the beginning. But for now, feast." He waved towards the angel's corpse. "Her flesh will make you strong."

Only Arandon held back as the others went to the body. Jacklin was the first to slice off a mouthful of the angel's flesh and swallow it down. The others followed quickly, then Rikkan's soldiers came forward to take their shares; a scrap of flesh to make the strong, a gulp of blood to make them immortal. Rikkan's elite, as bound to the cause as the Ertide's fellow Godless Kings.

"What are you doing?" Jertis asked.

Ertide had all but forgotten about his servant. The man was backed up against the wall, clutching his hands to his chest, his eyes wide and manic. Ertide took the jack from Arandon and approached.

Bind him.

"Drink, Jertis. Join us."

Jertis shook his head. "This is monstrous. Heresy. Madness. You... you killed her. You're eating her!"

"Drink, Jertis," Ertide said sharply, pushing the jack towards him. "Immortality. Take it. Join us." He had to. Ertide could not trust the man if he could not bind him.

Again Jertis shook his head. "I cannot, sire." He raised his eyes to the sky. "Oh God..."

Ertide dropped the jack and rushed forward. He slammed a hand underneath Jertis' jaw, slamming his mouth shut to cut off the prayer. Then he snatched the knife from his belt and buried it in Jertis' chest. The man met Ertide's gaze, still not understanding. He slid to the ground and died. Ertide stared down at the man who had served him for over a decade. He had a feeling Jertis would be only the first of many sacrifices.

He knelt by the body, slowly reached out and closed Jertis' eyes. "Damnit! Why couldn't you drink?" Ertide shook his head at the waste of it, of the man's life, but it had to be done. Anyone who wouldn't be bound might betray him. All it would take was one man to bring the rebellion to ruin.

He squeezed Jertis' hand gently. "I will take care of your family, Jertis. I promise. I will make sure they are safe."

Ertide strolled back to the angel corpse with Arandon at his side. The soldiers were busy carving bits off her. Oronesus was no longer identifiable as a person, an angel. She was just a body being sliced up. Meat and blood and bone, like any animal on the butcher's block.

The heart is where an angel's true power lies, Moon said.

"Give me the heart," Ertide said coldly.

Rikkan glanced up at him. His face was smeared with blood as he chewed on a strip of flesh. He, too, looked like an animal. They all did. He ripped open the ribcage, cracking bones, and cut the heart free, then held it up to Ertide. Ertide took it, held it in his hand for a few moments, staring into the lump of muscle that had so recently been the fire that kept Oronesus alive. Then he turned and held the heart out to Arandon.

"You are my heir, Arandon," Ertide said. "You know the truth. You saw through God's lies. If I fall, you are the one I charge with picking up my fight. Do not let us be enslaved again. Now take the power in this heart. Take it!" He dropped the heart into Arandon's hands.

As Arandon sank his teeth into the heart, Ertide glanced upwards. The sky was bright, cloudy but not threatening rain. It felt strange, like somehow after what they had just accomplished the day should have fled and given them the cover of night. Or maybe it just felt like day was the God's time and he might see them, their crime, from up in the blue sky at any moment.

Foolishness.

There was a Moon up there, though. He perched on the rooftop, black wings draped over his shoulders, blacker eyes staring hollowly, tears falling to the courtyard below. He looked right at Ertide, but he didn't see him. Moon's vision was elsewhere. Staring into the future. Watching the war that was to come.

CHAPTER 24

E*RTIDE LIMPED THROUGH THE PALACE HALLS USING HIS CANE* for support. It galled him to pretend at infirmity now he felt strong as an ox again, but the charade was important. It protected them all.

Moon strolled by his side, all smiles and jokes, tapping on the armour of soldiers they passed, fluttering his wings at passing servants to startle them. It was all a show. No one else saw it, but Ertide could see his friend was in pain. He was overcompensating with the frivolity.

No one remarked that Jertis was missing. Some noticed, surely, but they said nothing. His family had been told some story about a freak accident, a stray arrow during archery training. They would be taken care of. Ertide owed them that.

There were fewer soldiers about than usual. Nobody seemed to notice. Rikkan had long since replaced all the palace guard with his own personal crimson sashes. They had all been bound with angel blood. But their numbers had been reduced by Oronesus. The dead would need replacing soon, but by who? How could they trust anyone who hadn't been bound? An oath, perhaps?

They walked to the Grand Samir courtyard, the scene of the crime. From a balcony on the first floor, Ertide stared down at organised chaos. Already there was scaffolding in place, men and women rushing about, tools and materials being gathered. The architect Maud stood in the centre of it all, directing her people here and there. Ertide had chosen the four tiered garden with a hanging pond in the centre. Foolish extravagance, but it would hide the evidence. Oronesus' angelic emblem, an open tome with an archway scrawled across the pages, had been inked into the earth indelibly. They had tried to scrape the dirt away, but the lines went too deep. They had no choice, therefore, but to cover it. If the architect had thought the lines in the dirt strange, she had said nothing.

"It won't last," Moon said as he leaned against the balcony window and stretched out his arms. His eyes were clear again, for now, but Ertide could see the grief he was hiding. The first angel to die in two thousand years and Moon had orchestrated it, driven it. Enabled it. "The immortality you got from her blood, it won't last. It's not *true* immortality."

"Explain," Ertide said curtly.

"Each drop of her blood will heal a person of all their ills. It will extend their life by... I don't know. Years. But it's not immortality. Those extra years you took from her will eventually run out."

"Unless I take more." Ertide fingered the glass vial in his pocket, a few drops of angel blood suspended in alcohol solution.

Moon nodded sadly. "Unless you take more."

They both knew what that meant. Unless Ertide killed again. If he wanted to stay immortal, he needed to devour more angels.

After they had eaten their fill, they had carved Oronesus up, drained her dry, preserved what they could. Moon had said that the blood and flesh needed consuming within hours or it spoiled, and consuming spoiled angel would corrupt rather than empower. He'd provided them an alcohol solution that would preserve the blood and flesh's integrity for a while. What they had left would need using sparingly, to bind others to the cause. That was the only way Ertide could trust them.

He wondered what other properties angels carried in their bodies. Blood to extend life, flesh to make a person strong. The angel's heart gave a man power. What could he do with Oronesus' bones, her feathers, her hair? The butcher had worked for hours carving what he could and the blood had stained his hands a red that wouldn't wash off. *Passing odd*, he'd called it, a man who had worked with blood and corpses his whole life, now had hands stained crimson.

"How long do we have?" Ertide asked. "Before God finds out what we did."

Moon scoffed. "Not long if your fool of an heir keeps doing that in public."

Ertide leaned over the balcony to see Arandon standing below. He thought no one was watching and he held an open tome in one hand, his other hand hovering over it. He stared at the book with such concentration and slowly drew his finger to the side. The page raised laconically and then fluttered down again. Only a day since he had feasted on Oronesus' heart and already he was learning to use her power over paper.

Ertide cleared his throat loudly. Arandon startled and looked up, then snapped the book shut, turned and strode away. A gaggle of servants and guards raced after him.

All the responsibility of a king, but he wore no crown. *And he never will now. I am immortal. I am king. Forever.*

"How long do we have?" Ertide repeated.

Moon gave a dramatic shrug. "Impossible to say, old friend. How long do any of us have? How long before the moons fall from the sky? Before the seas rise to swallow us all? How long before the ancient terrors grow bored and come looking?"

"Moon!"

"Yes yes. Ignore the prophet when he starts spouting gibberish. I don't know. If God decides to look through Oronesus' eyes... he'll know she's gone. But she was always a bit of a dullard, head buried in books all the time, so maybe he won't bother. How long can you keep it a secret? What you did and what you are now? Hmm? How long before you need more?"

"Can't you see?" Ertide asked. "You know, look with your seer's sight."

Moon chuckled. "Are you asking me to, old friend?" He sounded scared. "I will, if you ask me too."

Ertide considered it. He knew what it cost Moon every time he used that sight, how difficult it was to find his way back to reality. Perhaps Moon had never told anyone else, but he had confided in Ertide. Navigating the myriad pasts and potential futures was like walking a tightrope, blindfolded, while carrying a bucket of water in one hand. So easy to fall. So easy to lose himself to the visions.

"No," Ertide said. "I won't ask you to do it."

Moon wheezed a ragged sigh. "Thank you. I don't know how long we have, old friend, but I do know we need to work quickly. You must make plans, gather weapons and allies, forge bonds. He will find out what we did, and when he does he will lay ruin to everything between you and him."

"How long do we have? Does it matter? Tell me, old friend. Do you think you will ever be ready to face the might of Heaven?"

Ertide had no answer to that. He had cured himself of his frailty, granted himself long life. But in doing so, had he also doomed them all? His family, his empire. Humanity.

"Oh look," Moon said, pointing to the sky. "The distraction has returned. Shame."

Ertide had to squint up into the bright blue sky. He saw a white blur, vaguely horse-shaped with expansive wings beating steadily at the air. Emrik had returned from Heaven.

"Are you coming?" Ertide asked as he turned and strode away from the balcony. The pegasus would land on the Sky Garden, and he intended to meet Emrik there. He fingered the vial of angel blood in his pocket again. He meant to bind Emrik to the cause, and then Merian, too.

"No," Moon said lazily, leaning against the window sill and staring down at the busy workers below. "I don't think I will."

"Suit yourself. Don't go disappearing on me this time, Moon."

He reached the door before Moon spoke again. "You can't trust him, old friend."

Ertide paused at the door and glanced back. Moon was still staring out the window.

"He's my grandson."

"And Caran is your son," Moon said.

"Both will come around. Especially once I bind them to the cause."

Moon turned dark eyes on him and gave a condescending shake of his head. "Talk to him, Ertide. Before you offer him anything, talk to him. Then decide."

Ertide left with a sour feeling curling through his stomach. Moon was always one to talk in vagaries and riddles, but this... *Maybe he's right? He hasn't been wrong about anything yet.*

The walk to the Sky Garden was painfully slow with his false infirmity. Ertide longed to stride, to run, but the ruse had to be kept where watchful eyes might see. The stairs, at least, were safe from outside scrutiny and he jogged up them happily. He almost felt young again. He would need to train in secret, build up some of the muscle he had lost.

By the time he reached the top of the Sky Garden he was sweating from the effort. He stooped his shoulders and bent his back, tucked his left hand into his jacket to feign uselessness, then limped out into the garden, leaning heavily on his cane.

The pegasus' hooves thrashed at the air as its wings beat their final approach. They truly were magnificent creatures. Beautiful and awe-inspiring. How he wished humanity could tame them for their own uses. Emrik leaned low on the beast's back, clinging to its mane. No pegasus would ever permit a saddle. It soared into the final approach and its hooves hit the stones with a clatter as it cantered to a stop, shook its wings, then folded them. The pegasus shook its head, turned to stare at Emrik with one eye, and snorted.

Emrik slid from the pegasus' back, stumbling on the flag stones and clutching at his crotch. "I hate you, beast," he said, wincing. "Whatever my sister sees in you, I don't know. If I had my way, you'd be steak."

The pegasus snorted again and reared up, spreading its wings so quickly it knocked Emrik to the ground. With a triumphant bray, the pegasus leapt into the air and flew away.

Emrik lay on the flag stones, watching the pegasus fly away. He flicked a rude gesture at it. "One day, I will eat pegasus steak."

Ertide ambled over to his grandson, his cane tapping the stone. Eleseth had not returned with Emrik, and Ertide was glad of that. He was worried if she tried to heal his pain away again, she might realise that he no longer suffered from any.

"Grandfather, you're walking!" Emrik shouted happily as he used a stone bench to pull himself back to his feet.

"Hah! Barely," Ertide said as he lowered himself carefully onto the bench. "At best, it's an arthritic stumble."

"Better than being pushed about in the chair by Jertis all day. Say, where is Jertis? I'd kill a leviathan for a mug of ale." He stretched out his arms, rolled his neck around until it cracked and popped, then pulled at his crotch again, wincing.

Ertide half pulled the vial out of his pocket.

Before you offer him anything, talk to him.

He clenched the vial in his fist. "So... Are you going to make me ask?"

Emrik grinned wide and opened his mouth to speak. The grin faded slowly and was replaced by a frown. He sat down heavily on the bench next to Ertide. He had his father's height, but wider shoulders and more meat to his frame. Ertide remembered him as such a scrawny little boy, but Emrik had grown into a giant of a man. Yet, his attitude never matched his physical presence. Some men filled a room just by walking into it. But not Emrik.

"So many times, my father has told me I was born in the wrong age," Emrik said. "I know he means it as an insult. I know he doesn't like me or respect me. He thinks I'm weak because I can't fight like him. It's his way of saying I should have been a poet, I guess. And we all know what the mighty Rikkan Hostain thinks of poets."

Ertide smiled at that. His son had been a bit of a poet himself when he was young. He liked to string words together in ways that didn't rhyme, but flowed. Until he'd discovered his true calling, his real passion. The blade.

"He's wrong, though," Emrik continued. "God told me he's wrong. Because what this age, the Fourth Age, needs isn't warriors and it isn't poets. It's adventurers, explorers. He said I have that spirit to me. The will to see the world and conquer it." He sounded strangely doubtful.

"God told you that?" Ertide asked.

Emrik nodded. "He let me in. I saw Heaven. Grandfather, you wouldn't believe..." Emrik glanced around, searching for something. "If I had paper and charcoal I could sketch you such a sight. It's beautiful. Everything gleams. The hallways and archways are carved with such mastery." He reached out a hand as if caressing something. "I don't have the words, grandfather. It's ancient, and wondrous, and... empty."

"Empty?"

Emrik nodded solemnly. "I thought it would be full of angels and pegasi and other creatures, but it's not. Heaven was empty. Like a palace with no guards, no servants, no people. Eleseth led me through the glowing halls, telling me stories of her siblings, of what the carvings on the doorways meant, but we saw no one. Not until...

"He was sat on a throne of golden light. The power that flowed from him, the presence. He filled it. Filled everything. The palace is empty because God fills it with himself." Emrik sighed and closed his eyes, leaning forwards as if exhausted just thinking about the encounter.

"I bowed, knelt. Did all the proper things. Don't worry, grandfather, I didn't embarrass us. But he stood from his throne and came close and... It was like being in the presence of the sun. So warm and bright and... at first it was comforting, like coming home from a hard day and being hugged by my wife. Hah! Or better yet someone who isn't my wife. But it was too much. He was too much. Too hot, too bright. It hurt just being near him."

Ertide rolled the vial of blood about in his fist. "What did he want from you?"

Emrik smiled, laughed. "He said this was my age. My age, grandfather. The Age of Exploration." The smile faded again, replaced with fear. "God wants me to lead the expedition. Mathanial's expedition. He wants me to sail away with the Rider and conquer the old world." Emrik turned a hollow stare on Ertide. "I'm to be king, grandfather. Not of Sant Dien. Of a new kingdom. A new empire I am supposed to build."

Ertide frowned. *A new empire. A house divided.*

"That is a lot of responsibility, Emrik."

His grandson nodded a bit too forcefully. "I know. I know. How the crap am I supposed to build a damn empire? But he said I was the one to do it. God said he believed in me. He told me his name, his true name. He said it was a measure of the trust he put in me."

God's true name? Ertide had never heard of that before. All the books, all his children, they all just called him God or father.

"What is it?" Ertide asked carefully. "God's name?"

Emrik glanced at him, his chubby, bearded face a picture of shock. "It's... It's..." He frowned, shook his head, opened his mouth, closed it again. "I can't say."

You can't trust him. That was what Moon had said. Ertide had been so quick to wave his friend's advice away. But there it was. Emrik had been taken to Heaven. He had knelt before God, before the enemy, and he had learned God's true name. And he kept it to himself.

Ertide slipped his hand back into his pocket and let go of the vial of angel blood.

I can't trust him. I cannot bind him, because he is already bound. Not to me. Not to the family or the empire. Emrik is bound to God.

AFTERWORD

Thank you so much for reading DEATHLESS and I do hope you enjoyed discovering how humanity fell from grace. If you did enjoy the book, please consider leaving a rating or review on Amazon, Goodreads, or any other platform you might frequent. Reviews are the lifeblood of books and you never know who you might inspire to give it a read.

And just a quick reminder that there are 2 companion trilogies being written alongside this one.

<u>The God Eater Saga</u> currently consists of:
    Herald (Age of the God Eater #1)
    Deathless (Annals of the God Eater #1)
    Demon (Archive of the God Eater #1)

While each trilogy can be read on its own, the saga is designed to be consumed together to get the best picture of the world, the story, and the characters.

Bound in blood!

Rob

BOOKS BY ROB J. HAYES

<u>The God Eater Saga</u> (Heroic Epic Fantasy)

Herald (Age of the God Eater #1)

Deathless (Annals of the God Eater #1)

Demon (Archive of the God Eater #1)

<u>The War Eternal</u> (Dark Epic Fantasy)

Along the Razor's Edge

The Lessons Never Learned

From Cold Ashes Risen

Sins of the Mother

Death's Beating Heart

<u>Titan Hoppers</u> (Coming of Age Sci-Fantasy)

Titan Hoppers

Spire Climbers

Fleet Champions

<u>The Mortal Techniques</u> (Asian Sword & Sorcery)

Never Die

Pawn's Gambit

Spirits of Vengeance

The Century Blade (short story)

<u>The First Earth Saga</u> (Grimdark Fantasy)

The Heresy Within (The Ties that Bind #1)

The Colour of Vengeance (The Ties that Bind #2)

The Price of Faith (The Ties that Bind #3)

Where Loyalties Lie (Best Laid Plans #1)

The Fifth Empire of Man (Best Laid Plans #2)
City of Kings

<u>It Takes a Thief...</u> (Lighthearted Steampunk)
It Takes a Thief to Catch a Sunrise
It Takes a Thief to Start a Fire